Cutters Cove

THE CARTEL

--- PULLING THREADS ---

Book Three

SHERYLL O'BRIEN

This is a work of fiction. All characters in this book are the product of an overactive imagination. Any businesses, organizations, places, events, and incidents are used fictionally. Any resemblance to a real person, living or dead, is a tremendous coincidence.

ISBN 978-1-939351-04-03

WOODWIND PRESS

Printed in United States of America

Mom,

I know that you think of me
every day of your life ---

I want you to know
how wonderfully comforting that is.

ACKNOWLEDGMENT

To my editor, Andria Flores, there is still no one else with whom I would want to go on this journey. Thank you for supporting my decision to bring these stories back to their original form – the novella. And thank you for your brilliance – not just in your editing work, but in the sparkle you bring to the world.

A heartfelt thank you to my team:

Andria Flores ~ Editor extraordinaire.
Nancy Pendleton ~ Goddess of the publishing world.
Jessica Champion ~ Web designer and manager.
25 Hours Consulting
Daryl Bruinsma ~ Cover Design & Animation.

Testimonials

"One book will set the hook!" ~ Nancy Pendleton

"This avid reader predicts that Sheryll O'Brien will become your favorite author. She's mine." ~ Ruth S. Bodreau

"The characters draw you in immediately. You will worry, laugh, hope, and love right along with them." ~ Donna Eaton

"There is nothing sweeter than a Sunday morning coffee, a blanket, overcast skies, and a *Pulling Threads* novel." ~ Andria Flores

"Everything you'd want in a good book. Humor, romance, suspense and great characters! It even takes place by the ocean! Loved it." ~ Helena Green

"I could write a book about the wonderfulness of it all." ~ Faith

"Hunks, humor, and heartache! What more could you ask for?" ~ Marjorie McCarthy

"*Bullet Bungalow* is a page turning family saga and then *Netti Barn* and *Cutters Cove* come along and add a whole lot of trauma to the drama." ~ Jessica O'Brien

"The most promising new author I've encountered in my publishing career!" ~ Jim P. - Woodwind Press

--- Pulling Threads ---

Bullet Bungalow
Netti Barn
Cutters Cove
They Run
They Hide
They Choose

Coming soon…

PENOBSCOT BAY
A Rocco Fiancetti Incorporated Investigation

Reasons
Rescues
Resolutions
Torment
Tango
Tests
Resolve
Revenge
Rebound

--- Twisted Threads ---

Coming soon…

Her Scream
Stay Safe

I hardly knew ye…
October

Fred gave Kitt's hand a gentle squeeze. She gave him a "deer caught in the highlights" look. She stepped to the casket of Joy Ann Watts and placed a single white rose onto the pale birch box. The perfect bud was beautifully tied with hand-embroidered ribbon that had been passed down through generations of Mahoney women. The Mahoney woman present that day chose a white rose and the white ribbon because…

Kitt took a moment for private reflection, then walked to the head of the casket and looked at the tiny group of mourners. The only people present that day were family and friends of Kitt, and yet it felt as though she were standing at Carnegie Hall in front of thousands of strangers, people who had gathered for a performance, for her performance. Kittridge Anne Mahoney was not at Carnegie Hall, she was at a centuries-old cemetery in Laurel Falls, Massachusetts, at the end of a barely paved lane, atop a tiny hill, at the freshly dug grave of a woman she barely knew—and didn't like all that much. Her role that day should have been nothing more than an attendee at the graveside service of Joy Ann Watts, and yet, there she was, at the head of the woman's casket readying herself to say a few words.

"There is very little that I know about Joy Ann Watts. I don't know what her favorite flower was or what her favorite color was. I don't know what her early years were like, or why she came to the choices she made in adulthood. I don't know if she was religious, or if she was guided by a higher spirit—but I do know this…

"Joy Ann Watts made sacrifices for the people she loved, and the nation she served. She put the wellbeing of others above her own, expected nothing in return, and shouldered her burdens in solitude. She did the right thing, even when it was the most difficult thing to do." **Kitt let an unexpected wave of loss and grief settle, then found the face of a teenage girl standing graveside. She offered a tiny smile, in lieu of the hug she wanted to give her. She received nothing in return, so…**

"The thought that I hold closest to my heart today, the thing that I believe most in my soul is this— Joy Ann Watts should have had the chance to know her daughter. Tess Maxwell should have had the chance to know her mother." **Kitt took a step away then stopped.** "I wish I had the chance to know Tess' mother, too."

Cutters Cove

Their daughter.

The last place Kitt Mahoney should be is sitting in the upstairs bedroom of her 14-year-old daughter, Tess. The only place she should be is at the Mahoney-Serpico Christmas Eve gathering that's in full swing one floor below. Bullet Bungalow, Kitt's beachfront home is brimming with people, all of whom are waiting for her to join them. There is one invited guest who has yet to arrive—she thinks his name is John Maxwell.

Kitt and John have been co-parenting friends for more than twenty years. For a dozen of those years, they shared their lives with their three daughters at a beautiful place called Netti Farmhouse in Mayflower, Massachusetts. It recently came to light that while Kitt was making memories, Liar-Liar-Pants-On-Fire was keeping secrets, undercover agent secrets, ABC sex tour secrets, God only knows what other kind of secrets. When the duplicity of John's life was revealed, the Mahoney-Maxwell clan was fractured, perhaps beyond repair.

For months now, John's words of confession have tormented Kitt's waking hours, and have shown no mercy from their nightly taunt...

"My name is John Maxwell. I own and operate a software design company called Netti Barn. My name is also Sam Sawyer. I am an undercover Federal agent working for an FBI cyber agency called FICA."

The betrayed woman is still pissed that her unwitting ass was dragged into Secret Agent Man's life, but she has decided to put her pain and anger to the side and move on. That's why she extended a voicemail invitation to John for Christmas Eve. The truth of the matter is, as mad as she is at him—she misses him. There is an even more pressing reason why Kitt invited John this evening—they share daughters—and one of them is hurting very badly. Tess, John's daughter with a woman named Joy, but raised by a woman named Kitt, hasn't seen, or spoken to her father in months. In fact, Tess has barely spoken to anyone for months—except for her dead mother, that is.

Every day, since early October, Tess has gone to Mayflower-Falls Cemetery and sat near the freshly packed grave of Joy Ann Watts. For several weeks, she uttered not a single word; she only cried. She talks to the grave now, and when she returns home, she says nearly nothing, which means her doppelganger sister, Callie, has no one to speak *unison* with. Both girls live under Kitt's roof 24/7 now, but there isn't a whole lot of living going on. Tess is carrying a world of hurt inside, and she needs help from those who love her—the thing is, she isn't feeling loved—she is feeling betrayed—as well she should.

It wasn't until her mother was dead and lying in a morgue in Mayflower, that the teen learned that: her parents maintained a secret relationship for fourteen years, that they both worked as undercover agents for the FBI for all of that time, that her mother recently spent several days hiding at her father's farmhouse, and that she died after being shot by a madman. That's some pretty heavy shit for a teenager, but the thing that rendered Tess mute was learning that her mother spent her last night alive sleeping in the girl's pink and white chevron wallpapered bedroom—the place where Kitt is sitting—on Christmas Eve—while there is a houseful of guests downstairs.

Try as she might, Kitt just can't get into the holiday spirit, but she can fake it—she's been faking it for weeks. After consistent prodding by her very handsome, very sexy, very significant other, Detective Fred Serpico, the two have been turning her beachfront bungalow into an icy wonderland.

"Fun and festive, that's what we're going for, Kittridge. Fun on the outside, that's my domain, and festive on the inside, that's your domain. Let's consider this a competition."

Kitt rolled her beautiful acorn-brown eyes, "Fred, is this really…"

"A competition? Yes, Ms. Mahoney, it is. Are you up for it?"

"Not really."

"But you don't know what you'll win—should you win."

"Okay, I'll bite, what will I win?"

"I'll take a dip in the ocean on New Year's Day."

"In swim trunks?"

"Yes."

"And no jacket, or socks, or mittens, or anything else?"

"That's right."

"And if you win?"

"I get you in bed with no jacket, or socks, or mittens, or anything else."

"Done."

It is Christmas Eve and the competition is underway. The outside of Bullet Bungalow can only be described as "fun". Sparkling silver things are hung and strung, here and there. Tiny twinkling icicle lights are wrapped around anything that doesn't move, and piped in, or in this case, piped out Christmas songs lift on

frosty air. Each of those are important design elements of Fred's domain, but…

"Fred."

"Yes."

"Why is the back of your truck full of snow?"

"Because we don't have enough at the bungalow."

"Do we need snow?"

"Yes."

"Why do we need snow?"

"You'll see."

When Kitt saw what Fred did with the trucked in snow, she was gobsmacked. "Snow people! Life-sized snow people! Fred Chester Serpico, you never cease to amaze."

Seated on the front porch, and lit by stationary ground lights, is an Honest Abe snow dude, with 3' tall stovepipe hat set upon his head, a wide smile stretched across his face, and a va-va-va-voom snow babe perched upon his lap. The snow version of the 16th President of the United States is leering at the snow babe's snow boobs—a rather easy thing to do since the snow w.o.m.a.n. is leaning back, smiling wide, and raising high one of Kitt's wineglasses in holiday cheer. Abe and Booby are true works of art, and worthy of a lengthy stare. They get them.

The walkway that leads to the backyard is lined with ice block molds that hold flickering votive candles set deep inside. Callie and Tess made them—well, it was Callie who made them, but Tess lit them this evening. All things considered that simple act is noteworthy. Around back, the porch is flanked on both sides with lighted tiki torches. Their flames flicker and reflect off of red, green, and gold tinted ice encrusted snow. The wave-like movements across the glittery landscape mesmerize the arriving and departing guests. All in all, Fred Serpico masterfully delivered on the "fun" but the question still remains: will he be taking home bragging rights, or will he be taking a dip in the Atlantic Ocean come New Year's Day? Time will tell.

It takes but one step inside Kitt's bungalow to know that the competition is on! The smell of warm apples and cinnamon, and the gentle waft of pine offer the guests their first embrace of Christmas. A crackling fire gently warms from a double-sided fireplace, the mantle of which is lined with white candles of all shapes and sizes, each one softly aglow. White Christmas stockings adorned with images of Santa doing this, or that, are hung from fireplaces, windowsills, and stair railings throughout the rooms. Shiny, silver bowls, overflowing with an array of take-home Christmas ornaments are set here and there, and shiny silver Santa sleighs brimming with leafy Poinsettia plants are tucked into corners.

All beautiful touches, indeed, but the "festive" is magnificently displayed by the seven-foot Douglas Fir that fills a corner of the living room. The perfectly shaped, and wonderfully fragrant focal point is lavishly decorated in frosty white lights and silver hanging ornaments. Laying beneath is a snowy white tree skirt, nearly every inch of which is covered with silver and white wrapped gifts. Christmas tunes, conversation, and laughter fill every corner of the holiday bungalow, and harken to the sequestered hostess who sits alone upstairs. Kitt knows that she should join in on the festivities, but she is tethered to the pink and white bedroom and imprisoned by the words of a woman who laid dying in her arms a few short months ago.

"John do list pink and white go deep Kitt thank you save Tess Fred message sorry save list Annie system crashed."

Joy Ann Watts uttered those incoherent words moments after she took a bullet to the back.

Joy trained her eyes on the loft and watched as the madman surveyed the scene.

He had Annie wedged tight between him and the window. "He's focused on the outside. That means that he doesn't know John and Fred are inside the barn. They have a chance. What's he doing? What's he looking for?" A flicker from the window pulled Joy's attention, clarified the moment. It all happened in a split second—she saw Hector position his rifle—she jumped in front of Kitt, shielding her from Hector's bullet. The women hit the ground wrapped in each other's arms.

Kitt pains with the knowledge that Joy is the woman who should be sitting in that bedroom on Christmas Eve getting to know her 14-year-old daughter, Kitt's daughter—their daughter.

Was she pretty?

John Maxwell is dragging his ass to a Christmas Eve gathering at Bullet Bungalow. After recent events and revelations, he was surprised that he received an invitation—unhappily surprised. In every way imaginable, he would rather skip this evening's event. He knows he can't. His attendance is mandatory, a part of his penance, a very small part, and the first of many to come. There is another reason why John is heading to the bungalow, a very important reason, her name is Tess.

"Have you given it any thought?" He crossed the room and wrapped his arms from behind her, his hands gently meeting at the front of Joy's full-term baby belly.

"You should name her, John."

"I'll be raising her. Do this for her, do it for yourself."

"Tess," she whispered.

"Tess," he repeated. "So you *have* given it thought," he smiled. "I haven't heard that name before."

"I read it in a book. *Tess of the d'Urbervilles*, by Thomas Hardy."

"Tess," he repeats it. "I like it. I wonder if it means something."

"To harvest. To reap. To gather."

He kissed her neck, pulled in the fruity-smell of her hair, "Yeup, you've given it lots of thought. I'm glad you did, Joy."

On autopilot now, John travels the length of Farm Road, to Main Street, then along the quiet and quaint avenues of the seaside village of Mayflower. He barely notices the thirty foot tree in the center of town, or the Christmas lights strung from one lamppost to the next, to the next, to the next. When his senses return, he finds that he's arrived in neighboring Laurel Falls, and has parked his SUV at the entrance of Mayflower-Falls Cemetery. He wonders if he should go in. "Nope," he quickly decides. He starts his car just as tiny snowflakes start falling. Before long they've covered his windshield, the wipers slowly tracking across the glass, sweeping away the tiny crystals. Still parked at the iron gates, he gets lost in thought, once again.

"AH! You'd better run!"

Her aim was perfect. He would have taken the snowball square to the face had he not turned. As it was, it landed somewhere between his cheek and chin, the majority of it sliding down into the collar of his pea coat. He set off after her, closing the space between them in three or four steps. He wrapped his arm around her waist and pulled. They tumbled to the ground with her on top of him, until he rolled her beneath.

"Joy," the word low and husky.

"You love me," she beamed.

"Yeup. What gave it away?"

"You brought me to Mayflower to meet your family."

"You are my family." He pulled a quick breath, and kissed her. And just as she always did, she took his breath away.

John banged his hand angrily against the steering wheel. "God dammit, Joy."

Bullet Bungalow

Fred meets John on the driveway. The men haven't seen one another since the formal inquest of the October shooting that took place at Netti Barn. Fred offers his hand in greeting, "Good to see you, John."

"You, too, Fred. The place looks nice."

"It was an all-hands-on-deck kinda thing. Tess and Callie made the ice candles. Didn't think it could be done, but they proved me wrong."

John takes a long look at the flickering flames, "How is she, Tess, I mean?"

"Quiet. Although she's coming around a bit. The holidays are helping. She still walks to the cemetery every day and sits on the grave, sometimes for hours. I'm kinda glad it's getting too cold for her to stay out as long as she has been."

John leans back against the SUV and hangs his head.

Fred almost doesn't ask his next question. Fred's a detective, so he asks his next question, "Have you been to Joy's grave, yet?"

"No."

Fred taps John's shoulder. "Come on. Let's get this over with."

The men silently follow the ice candle trail toward the backyard. Fred enters the bungalow. John remains on the porch.

That's where Kitt finds him nearly an hour later. "John."

"Kitt."

As though they share a single thought, they move to the porch sofa. Kitt kicks off her ankle boots and pulls her feet up beneath her thighs, as she is wont to do. She pulls her coat tight and tries to hug away the shivers that quickly grab hold. For a couple of minutes they look out at the backyard, each one caught by the reflective flame show, and by their own thoughts. She reaches for his hand, and pulls it onto her lap, "Would you like to come inside?"

He gently gives her hand a squeeze, "I know I should, for Tess, but..."

She nods her understanding, "I know. Tonight is a challenge for me, too. I only managed to come downstairs a half-hour ago, and I'm hosting this damn thing."

He smirks. She offers one of her million-watt smiles, granted it's missing nearly all of its watts, but still. Kitt leaves John to his thoughts, and heads inside. As she mingles here, and flits about there, she peeks out at the near-broken man. He spends most of his time standing and staring at the dark ocean, and bits of time suffering through holiday pleasantries with guests who are heading home. When the last of the Christmas Eve gatherers have gone, Tess steps to the back door.

"Dad."

He turns. "Hey, Tess," the name caught on an exhale.

"You should come inside. It's beautiful and warm. There's lots to eat and Mom..." Tess pauses, suddenly unsure about the word, but quickly continues, "Mom made that warm apple cider thing you love."

The expectant hope on his daughter's face hits where it should. "Sure, Tess. That sounds nice."

Callie, Fred, and Kitt busy themselves with kitchen cleanup, as Tess and John head through to the living room. He finds his way to the tree, and immediately gets lost in his thoughts, again. After a few minutes, Tess gets up from the couch and joins him there. Kitt stands in the doorway and watches a father and a daughter inch their way back to one another.

"They're pretty," she whispers.

"What?"

"The ornaments. They're pretty," she repeats.

"Yes, very pretty."

A few minutes pass before Tess speaks again, "Was Mom, I mean Joy, was she pretty?"

Before John can answer, Kitt joins them at the tree and points to a gift, "Tess, that's for you. I think now is the perfect time for you to open it."

Fred and Callie join them in the living room, standing quietly off to the side. All watch as Tess pulls a silver tie from a shiny white gift-wrapped box, moves aside silver tissue paper, and removes a black framed picture. She stares at the photo, then looks back and forth between John and Kitt.

"Is this a picture of Joy?" she chokes through tears. Kitt sweeps hair from Tess' shoulder and looks deeply into her tear-filled eyes.

"It's a picture of your mother," she says as she moves her hand next to John's. When he takes hold, she whispers, "Partners," as she's done hundreds of times before.

"Always."

I couldn't stay away.

Annie Mahoney-Maxwell, is sitting in her Jeep Wrangler in the parking lot of a sea weathered wood and red brick condo building in a sleepy corner of Mayflower. The man that Annie was falling in love with lives in that building—he nearly died in that building—she nearly died right along with him. Annie is tortured by the memories of that night in October—the truth is, Annie is torturing herself.

"Dad. Fred. Please come." Her tremble was worsening and she was losing whatever control she had. The mantra, her lifeline, tumbled on a whisper, "Dad. Fred. Please come. Dad. Fred. Please come. Dad…" The repeated droning of those words, and the effects of the chloroform her kidnapper used to subdue her, helped fuel a powerful fatigue. Just as she was surrendering to sleep's protective pull, a growing sense of dread hit her **hard**. "Mike." Tears filled her eyes as she remembered that Mike was her protection. He wouldn't let anyone take her. He would have protected her with his life. That's what he tried to do that night.

The Mayflower-Falls police officer was shot at pointblank range when he opened his condo door expecting to find his partner, Grant

Speil, on the other side. What he found instead was the gun of a madman pointed at his chest. Mike was critically wounded during that encounter. "Is there a Detective Fred Serpico here?" a nurse in surgical scrubs asked.

"I'm Detective Serpico."

"I have your name as contact person for Officer Michael Monopoli. He is in critical condition in the Surgical ICU. If you have contact information for his next of kin, you should be in touch with them…"

Annie blames herself for what happened that night, it's why she stays away from the man she wants, the man she needs. "Mike." She says his name, says it again, "Mike." Call it a Christmas Eve miracle, or the reappearance of a tenacious woman who's been on hiatus, but the simple act of saying his name sets her free. Annie Mahoney-Maxwell finds the truth of the matter, "I am not to blame for Mike's shooting— well, not singularly to blame for it, anyway. Oh, for fucks sake. What is wrong with me? Hector shot Mike – to get to me – to get to my father. Hector is to blame. John Maxwell – or Sam Sawyer – or whoever the spy is today is to blame." Annie straightens in her seat and continues her roll, "I made my share of mistakes, but the biggest mistake, the one that matters most, is my staying away from Mike." The fired up young woman grabs her keys from the ignition, gets out of her Jeep, slams its door shut behind her, storms across the parking lot, up the walkway, and to the buzzer pad. She pushes the button for 2A, pushes it a second time. When no answer comes, the heavyhearted young woman whispers the words she would have said had Mike been there to hear them, "I'm sorry." Her heart lifts when he responds.

"Annie! Is that you?" Mike yells into the speaker.

Just hearing his voice undoes her resolve, she drops to her knees, unable to answer. She wraps into herself and breaks—the emotional release a long time in coming.

Mike pulls his condo door wide, and bolts across the second floor toward the stairway. The commotion would normally have resulted in a hall full of nosey neighbors, but the floor is abandoned this Christmas Eve. Mike takes the stairs two at a time, and when he pushes into the vestibule he finds that he is unable to open the door—Annie is pressed tight against it from the other side. Clad only in jeans and a partly-open sweatshirt, his shoulder strapped tightly by a stability brace, he runs down the hall, pushes open a side door, props it with a trashcan, and runs around to the front stair landing. "Annie," he squats and puts his good arm around her shoulders.

She trembles beneath his touch.

"Annie. Can you get up? It's freezing out here. If we don't get moving, I'm gonna need your help in a minute."

His words hit home. She looks up, and notices his braced shoulder for the first time. "Mike." The whispered word is filled with agony. She pulls in the last of her ragged breaths, then pulls herself upward. He wraps his good arm around her back and leads them to the side door. Once inside, they awkwardly wrap around one another. "Mike. I shouldn't have left."

The last time Annie saw Mike, he was in an ICU bed, barely clinging to life. "You should talk to him," the ICU nurse encouraged her.

"What should I say?"

"You've been here every day for a week. Tell him that. Then tell him the important things."

When she was alone, Annie took hold of his hand, pressed it to her cheek, and whispered, "Please come back, Mike. I need to finish falling in love with you." She stayed by his side for several more days, but when he finally opened his eyes—she was gone.

Mike and Annie quietly make their way to 2A. He helps her with her coat and leads her to his bedroom. She sits on the edge of his bed and begins shivering.

"Your pants are soaked. You need to get out of them." The young officer, the man trained to protect and serve, pulls open a bureau drawer revealing the things Annie brought with her during the Hector nightmare. Though she never returned after the kidnapping and shooting, he settled her clothes for the long haul—where they have lain, waiting for her to come back to claim them. Annie walks to Mike, wraps her arms around him, and snuggles against his back. He turns to her, sweeps her long hair from her shoulder, gazes deeply into her gold-flecked, acorn-brown eyes, and sees something that hasn't been there before. Surrender. Annie has stopped fighting her feelings for him and has taken down her walls. For the first time, Mike knows that Annie is his. He kisses her just to be sure. He is sure.

Annie Mahoney-Maxwell is with Michael Monopoli. Finally, with Mike. A smile warms her as she gathers things to change into. Being with him is what she's wanted and needed for months. And here it is Christmas Eve and—"Oh! Shit! Mom's Christmas Eve gathering! Oh, Shit. What time is it?"

"Almost eleven."

"I need to make a call." It goes directly to voicemail. "Mom, I'm with Mike." Annie says nothing more—nothing more needs to be said.

After showering and slipping into a pair of pajama bottoms and tank top, Annie returns to an empty bedroom. She sets out looking for Mike, stops short when she enters the living room. Nestled in a back corner of the open floor living room is a beautifully decorated Christmas tree. Set nearby is a double-wide, micro-suede recliner upon which Mike sits. She raises a brow in question, first to the tree, then to the recliner.

"The tree is courtesy of Cluster and Jane. They said I needed some Christmas cheer. I accepted it on the condition that they remove it right after New Year's Eve. As for the recliner," Mike points to his shoulder, "I can't put pressure on it, so I can't sleep in a bed. This is very comfortable and lots of fun. Try it out."

Annie humors the injured man. He gets up - she gets on - and is immediately swallowed by the behemoth.

"You look like Goldilocks in Papa Bear's chair."

She rubs the soft suede, "Yeup, this is j.u.s.t. r.i.g.h.t."

He laughs, "Better than just right, it rocks, reclines, vibrates, and heats up," he says as he heads to the kitchen.

"Then I guess I won't be needing you for anything," she laughs.

He growls on his way back with two glasses of wine. "I hope the pajama set means that you'll stay the night."

Annie gets off the recliner. Mike sits down. Annie joins him, nestling tight against his good side. She takes a sip of wine, pulls a deep breath, and relaxes into the moment. In the deepest places of her heart, Annie knows that she belongs with Mike. Always with Mike.

Just before she falls asleep, he whispers, "You were there."

"Where?"

"The ICU. I could feel you. I fought dragons to get back to you, Sweet Annie. When I woke up you were gone."

He pulls her close and relaxes for the first time since the shooting. Before he falls asleep, he whispers. "Annie."

"Hmm?"

"Why did you leave?"

"I couldn't stay."

"Why did you come back?"

"I couldn't stay away."

Merry Christmas to me.

Kitt Mahoney wakes Christmas morning to an empty bed. She finds her man across the room, staring out a window at the Atlantic Ocean. She quietly enjoys a few minutes of his naked form. *Merry Christmas to me.*

Detective Fred Serpico is an intelligent, intuitive, and fiercely loyal man—he is also a **very** handsome man. He is tall and built, with broad shoulders and tucked abs. Definitely on the sinewy rather than bulky side of strong. He has black, somewhat wavy hair, moss green eyes, is rarely clean shaven, preferring a neatly trimmed scruff, and he has long, line dimples that cut his cheeks when he smiles—which is often. Kitt can tell from Fred's posture that he is not smiling. Whenever the detective needs to process, he stares out of whatever window is available. The fact that he is standing and processing on Christmas morning is worrisome. "This can't be good," she offers from the toasty warmth of her California king.

When Fred turns toward Kitt, she is busily tucking errant strands of her long, wavy hair into a messy bun. Every time she pulls her hair up and away from her face, Fred gets intense. "I'd set you right this morning, Ms. Mahoney, but you're still flush from last night's go around."

She adds a blush to her flush at the memories of his Christmas Eve debauchery, then pulls free from the sheets that cover her from the waist down. She pats the bed, "You can stay looking out that window, Fred, or—" her eyes follow the length of her man as he crosses the room. He places one knee onto the bed and pulls her beneath him. She squeals with delight as he presses her deep into the mattress and works her girly bits.

"Kittridge," he moans as he enters her, and tenderly brings her toward a lovely Christmas orgasm.

"Oh, Fred, it's just what I always wanted," she pants through her release.

Cutters

Annie Mahoney-Maxwell wakes alone on the behemoth Christmas morning. Mike is across the room, staring out a slider at an overcast sky and churning Atlantic Ocean. "Hey Monopoli, what's so interesting?"

He moans at the sound of her voice and drops his head, "Go back to sleep, Annie."

"Is something wrong? Are you angry?"

"No, I'm just—" When he turns her way, he's sporting a **very** noticeable piece of unfinished business.

Annie giggles and pats the recliner, "You can stay looking out that window, Mike, or—"

Mike plants his feet firmly in place, a painful groan escapes him. "I should probably stay here, Annie. I don't think I could stop this time. I want you pretty bad."

"I see that. Don't plan on stopping this time. If it's okay with you, I mean if it's okay with your shoulder and all, I'd sort of like to see what all the sexual noise is about."

Mike would have gone airborne if he could have. Instead, he stalks toward Annie, stripping off his sweats along the way. The perfectly cut hunk stops when he gets to the behemoth, "Are you still on the pill?"

"Not that I've needed it, but yes."

"Stand up, Annie, on the chair."

Annie's 5'2" frame sinks a bit in the cushiony recliner, but still she's slightly taller than Mike.

"Top," he says.

Annie removes her tank.

He moans. "Bottoms," he says.

She removes her pajamas, but leaves on her thong, purely for tease.

He moans. "Thong," he begs.

"So far, I'm liking the noise," Annie teases.

Mike swings his good arm around her waist, "Climb onto my hip, then wrap your legs." He groans again when their flesh meets. He lowers their bodies onto the recliner and sort of growls when Annie straddles him and eases him in.

"Merry Christmas to me," Annie tightens and whimpers.

Bullet Bungalow
Tess Maxwell wakes Christmas morning with the eyes of a mother she never knew upon her. She examines the picture under dreary, overcast morning light. "You are really pretty," she corrects herself, "You were really pretty. You look like Amanda Seyfried."

The picture that Tess has is of a really happy Joy. Her blonde hair is cropped short, the longest part skimming the nape of her neck. Her piercing blue eyes are lushly lashed and her smile is wide and expressive. Tess touches a tiny teardrop dimple under Joy's eye then touches her own. "I got this from you," she sighs. She stares for several minutes, then takes the note that was tucked inside the gift box.

> Dear Tess,
> I think you should have this picture. It was taken fifteen Christmases ago during a winter sleigh ride in Mayflower. It is of your parents from a time when they were happily in love. I spent a few days with your mother during that Christmas week, and I liked her very much. She was warm and very approachable, and had a big, expressive laugh. And she could put your father in his place, which I particularly enjoyed. When I met Joy again, I could tell that she was conflicted by her life choices. She spent her last night alive at Bullet Bungalow sleeping in your room. She wanted to

know you in the only way she could at that moment. I believe your mother would have connected with you had she been given more time. I'm sorry that she wasn't.
Love, Mom

Tess brings a finger to her lips, kisses it then reaches out and places the kiss on her mother's lips. "I wish I met you, Mom."

Mayflower-Falls Cemetery
John Maxwell wakes Christmas morning at the base of a small hill in a cold, barren graveyard. He's been in his SUV since he left Bullet Bungalow the night before. When he entered the cemetery he expected—he hoped—that he would feel *something*.

"It's been months. Why don't I feel it? Am I that fractured of a human being that I can't even..." He waits for the pain of loss—he settles for feelings of shame. "I let you be buried alone. I let Tess mourn her mother alone. I let Kitt shoulder those burdens alone."

The man who wreaked havoc in everyone's lives hasn't owned any of it. He certainly hasn't told his 14-year-old daughter anything about her mother's life or her death. At first, he blamed that failure on the silence that grabbed hold of them. That of course was bullshit. John Maxwell didn't talk to Tess because he couldn't. He was too damned pissed at Joy Ann Watts. Pissed that she missed out on knowing their daughter. Pissed that she chose FICA over him, over them. Pissed that she died.

"John," Kitt's voice heavy with pain. "Any news on Joy?"

"She's in the OR. Her condition is critical. She's fighting," he said, although he didn't know that to be true. Admittedly, he didn't know anything. "What happened?"

Kitt shook her head, "I'm not sure exactly. Hector wedged Annie against the window. Joy mumbled a few things about you and Fred being inside the barn, then a shiny flash came from the loft, and before I knew it, Joy tackled me, and we hit the ground. She was mostly on top of me, and when I tried to get out from under her, my hands got covered in…and Joy started mumbling…and…"

The cold, angry man is suddenly filled with the urge to tell Joy what he thinks—he reaches for the door handle then pulls back. He doesn't open the door and walk up that small hill to be with Joy. Instead, he starts his SUV and leaves Mayflower-Falls Cemetery. His parting words falling on deceased ears, "I wish I never met you, Joy."

You gonna tell me what this means?

Detectives Serpico and Phelps are not scheduled to work the day after Christmas, but Fred needs to talk. Some things have been banging in his head for more than a month, and he needs a sounding board. Detective Steve Phelps is the best sounding board Fred knows. The thing is, Steve isn't expected at the station for another twenty minutes, so Fred does what he always does when he's in the office. He stares out the window overlooking the main streets of Mayflower, and processes.

"This can't be good," Steve says, when he enters the office. "We're not even working a case, and you're processing the shit out of something."

"I've been thinking..."

"You're always thinking. Don't you ever sleep?"

"Not lately." Fred takes one final look out the window and begins. "I told you that Kittridge has been upset by the whole, *Joy took a bullet that was meant for her* thing."

"Yeah."

"That's only part of the story, Steve."

His partner kicks back in his chair, puts his feet on his desk, and his hands behind his head.

It's his signal that Fred has his complete attention. "Tell the story, Fred."

"When Joy was bleeding out in Kittridge's arms, she said some things that didn't make any sense..."

"Sorry for the interruption Fred, I know how much you hate that, but Joy was dying. Chalk up whatever she said to blood loss and confusion."

"I did."

"But you don't, anymore?"

"Nope," Fred reaches into his jeans pocket and pulls out a slip of paper. "I wrote down what Joy said in the order that she said it. Kittridge told me that Joy chopped the words out on exhales, really struggled to finish." Fred hands the paper to Steve. He reads it out loud.

"John do list pink and white go deep Kitt thank you save Tess Fred message sorry save list Annie system crashed." He pauses then asks, "You gonna tell me what this means?"

Fred turns back to the window, "What if those words hadn't been chopped out on a dying woman's breath. What if the words are part of a sentence or a story?"

Steve looks at the paper, again. "Give me more, Fred. Connect this for me."

"Let's take it step-by-step. (John do list). We know that John and Joy were following a list of destinations for their yearly ABC reunions. We also know that Joy never made it to Madrid, this year's location, because Hector started the *unmask me, or I kill Sam Sawyer game*. What if there's a reason Joy wants John to continue doing the ABC list?"

Steve shrugs. Fred Continues.

"(Pink and white). Joy spent her last night alive in Tess' bedroom. I think that's Joy's reference…"

Steve jumps in, "Joy slept in Tess' room— the night the shit hit the fan about John being a Fed? That night? How'd that happen?"

"Kittridge thought Joy might like to get to know Tess a bit, so she told Joy to spend the night in her room."

Steve shakes his head, brushes imaginary lint from his jeans, "Damn, Fred. That woman of yours never ceases to amaze."

"Don't I know it," Fred pauses a minute before resuming. "(Go deep). That's where cyber geeks go when they do their cyber stuff. Maybe there's a reason someone should (go deep). To be honest, I need help on this one. We'll come back to it. (Kitt thank you save Tess). Kittridge said that those words were grouped together, like it was one complete thought, but…" He ponders a bit, "At first, I thought it was a stated thank you to Kittridge for saving Tess, but Kittridge didn't save Tess, she raised her. Now I think the important part of (Kitt thank you save Tess) is (save Tess). I'm convinced this is a plea, a directive that someone should save Joy's daughter, Tess."

Right on cue, Steve kicks his feet off his desk, gets up, and starts pacing. His partner gives him more to pace about.

"(Fred message). I instantly knew what this meant. When I got the call that morning from Cluster saying Monopoli had been shot and Annie was missing, I called out to John, Joy, and Kittridge to join me in the kitchen. John was in the living room and Kittridge was in her bedroom, so they came immediately. It took longer for Joy to come because she was upstairs in Tess' room. I barked out what the situation was with Monopoli and Annie and almost simultaneously John got an alert that Netti Barn was breached. He and I were scrambling to get out the door when Joy grabbed hold of my arm and said, 'Fred, I need to tell...' She was cut off by John in his urgency to get out, and she let go of my arm, but she sent me a look of utter desperation. Joy needed to tell me something, and the longer I sit with all of this, I'm convinced it was something big."

"Maybe she wanted to go with you guys. Hector was her nemesis, too."

"I thought that's what it was, but Kittridge said that Joy had no intention of following us to Netti Barn. When Kittridge forced the issue with Joy, she said she still wouldn't budge. Special

Agent Watts was going to follow Special Agent Maxwell's order for them to stay at the bungalow. Joy only left that morning because Kittridge said she'd have to shoot her to keep her from leaving. That's when Joy caved."

"Huh."

"Special Agent Watts wasn't obligated to follow Special Agent Maxwell's directive, they were of equal authority in a situation like that. But according to Kittridge, Joy was gonna sit still at the bungalow."

"Huh."

"You already said that."

"It needs repeating."

Fred nods. Fred continues. "Next up on the death-mumble is (sorry). Let's consider this your standard, 'I'm dying' statement, so that brings us to (save list Annie system crashed). Let's break this into two pieces, (save list) (Annie system crashed). Maybe something needs to be saved and the list is key. Again, this needs work. (Annie system crashed). I have no clue. I do know that we need to talk to John and Annie about (go deep) and (system crashed)."

Steve is full-out pacing the room. "Jesus, Fred, do you think that's smart? I mean, John's practically a hermit, and Annie's PTSDing all over the place from Alden and Hector. What are you thinking, man?"

"I'm thinking Kittridge is pregnant."

Steve's pacing stops on a dime. A huge grin crosses his face, "Shit, Fred, you probably should have started with that news."

As though she'd seen a ghost.

     Tess is creeped out. For the very first time since she's been going to her mother's grave, she is scared. Correction: she is terrified. This is particularly upsetting because not only has the teen felt safe at the tiny cemetery, she's found a peaceful way to connect with her mother. That is **so** not the case right now.

     Tess Maxwell scans the beautiful, but barren place of eternal rest. She is sure that she'll find someone lurking about, she hopes otherwise. "Please don't let anyone be here." She **knows** someone is there. She takes another look around. "Please let it be another visitor. Please let it be someone walking their dog." She finds no one, only gravestones, monuments, and a groundskeeper's shack. She assesses, "Those are big enough for someone to hide behind." She shivers—not from the frigid cold, but from the worst case of heebie-jeebies she's ever had. She wants to get up and leave, or scream out the panic she's holding back, but she is frozen by fear. Relief bangs hard when she hears the purr of an engine in the distance. The terrified teen turns toward the sound, her eyes fill at the sight of Annie's orange Jeep inching its way down the narrow, barely paved roads. Tess bolts from the bench upon which she's been perched and races toward her sister. She practically rips off the Jeep's door and throws herself inside.

"Are you alright, Tess? God, you look like you've seen a ghost. I suppose that's possible considering where we are, but..."

"No! I mean, yes. I mean, can we get out of here? Now, please!"

Annie speeds from the cemetery, her eyes locked on the skinny pathways she quickly navigates. If she had looked around, she would have seen the source of her sister's fear. It wasn't a ghost.

Bullet Bungalow

Kitt is in the kitchen, "banging pots". That's her way of saying she's cooking rather than heating something up. She's adding a generous helping of parboiled potatoes and carrots into a crockpot stew when her girls race in from outside. "Whoa, whoa, what's gotten into you two?" She looks back and forth, expecting one of them to speak, and since Tess isn't in a speaking mood, she expects Annie to speak.

"I'm not exactly sure," she begins, "I swung through the cemetery like I always do to see if Tess wanted a ride home, and she was all freaked out. She threw herself into the Jeep as though she'd seen a ghost."

Kitt goes to her daughter and brushes her honey-colored curls from her ashen face, "Tess, what happened?"

"Nothing. I was just freaked out. There wasn't anyone there, I looked around."

"Just because you didn't see anyone doesn't mean someone wasn't there," Annie counters.

"Did you see anyone?" Kitt asks Annie.

"No, but I was driving."

Tess squeezes her eyes tight, "May I go upstairs?"

"Sure, I'll call you for dinner. It will be about an hour or so. Try to rest a bit."

Annie waits until Tess is on the stairs before pushing in, "Mom, Tess was *freaked out*. I've **never** seen her like that. When she saw my Jeep, she bolted from the bench at Joy's grave and ran so fast, I thought she might fall down the hill. It's small and all, but there are headstones and monuments everywhere. Maybe Tess shouldn't go to the cemetery alone anymore."

"I'll talk to her, really try to figure out why she became so unsettled, today. I agree with you, though, she should curtail her trips if she doesn't have someone with her."

Annie starts toward her mini master, "Annie Mahoney-Maxwell, a word please." Kitt's oldest daughter, the one who would be a snarling pit bull right now, smiles pleasantly knowing full well that this conversation could go off the rails at any time. "You left here on Sunday. It's Tuesday. Explain yourself."

"I've been at Mike's."

"Yes, I already know that part of the story."

"We're trying things out."

Kitt raises a curious brow.

"Not like that. Well, not only like that," Annie smirks, spins on her heels, and calls over her shoulder, "Let's do this again, sometime."

The mother calls after the daughter, "Do I need to lecture you about safe sex, Annie Mahoney-Maxwell?"

The daughter who was conceived while the mother was still in high school stops at the entrance of her mini and laughs her next words, "You? You want to lecture me about safe sex? That's priceless, Mom."

"Point taken," she concedes.

Netti

John's SUV is parked in the driveway when the MFPD detectives arrive. The farmhouse is completely dark, so they head to the barn. It is closed tight and looks as though it has been that way for quite a while. They head back to the house and knock, several times. Fred calls John from his cell, pocketing it without leaving a message. After a few more knocks, Fred leans against the doorbell and points to a glass panel in the back door.

Steve shakes his head, "Fred don't. He could be out with someone, or he doesn't want to come out and play, right now. Let's come back tomorrow..." The logical detective hasn't finished his sentence, when it is cut short by the breaking of glass followed by the immediate shrill of an alarm.

Within seconds, John stumbles to the door and begins punching in alarm codes. The look on his face suggests that he wants to punch a few other things. "What the fuck?" He pulls open the back door, then a utility door, and tosses Fred a broom and Steve a dustpan. "Clean it."

The detective holding the broom notices the slurring of words and a vacant look on the homeowner's face, "Are you drunk?"

"No. I was asleep. For the first time in weeks, I might add. Why are you here, and what's with the breaking and entering?"

"Technically, it's only breaking, John. You allowed the entering by opening the door."

"Fred, I'm about to pass out from exhaustion. What do you want?"

"I want to figure out if Tess is in danger, and I need your help."

John reaches into the front pocket of his jeans and pulls out a prescription bottle. He tosses it to Fred, "You'd better take these with you then, and give me eight hours to sleep off the pills I already took."

Bullet Bungalow
Fred passes Annie on her way out, "Where are you heading?"

"Mike's."

Fred points to Annie's suitcase and duffle bag, "You moving out?"

"Not yet," she winks.

"Tell Mike to keep it safe."

"Right backatcha, Serpico."

Fred playfully bellows when he enters the kitchen, "Kittridge, what is that amazing smell?"

She leaves the bedroom on a yawn and runs her hands through a mess of waves.

"Were you sleeping?"

"I must have dozed off for a few minutes. Did you just get in?"

"Yeah. I ran into Annie on the driveway. I think she's moving out."

"Eventually, I think. I know it's fast and all, but she and Mike have been through some major things already and have made it to the other side. I'm happy for them."

Fred pulls Kitt into his arms. She yawns in his face.

"You feeling alright?" he asks.

"Fine. What's with that weird smile on your face?" she nudges.

"I thought you liked my smile," he nudges.

"Not this one," she snaps.

He laughs big.

Callie and Tess join Fred and Kitt for dinner. Two of the diners eat—the other two pick at their food. Kitt has already had her fill during the "banging pot" session, so she doesn't need any more to eat. Tess is obviously still upset from the graveyard incident, and can't eat. Fred shoots Callie a questioning look. She tosses an unknowing shrug. Fred tosses two ten dollar bills onto the table. "Cleanup is on you two, okay?"

The girls nod and pocket the money.

The man on a mission enters the master only to find that the woman he seeks has abandoned it. He follows the sounds of running water and a very off-key rendition of *Oh! Darling*. She startles when he opens the door and thrills when he strips and joins her. A shiver runs from tip to toe as his hand moves up her soapy thigh, then the length of her. He gently tilts her head back and indulges with a soul-searing kiss. He steps back and traces his fingertips along her jaw, down her neck to the swell of her breasts. He stops his affectionate exploration at her abdomen where he traces a tiny swelling, "Kittridge," he flattens his palm across her stomach, calling attention to the swell, "are you pregnant?"

She smacks him across his shoulder, "Of course, I'm not pregnant."

"But this," Fred rubs the bit of a bud.

She laughs and smacks him again, "That's a stew belly, Fred, but thanks for calling attention to it." She leaves the frustrated man alone in the shower to ponder his stupidity. She is still giggling as she makes her way to the bedroom to dress. When she nears the home office, she stops for a thought or two, then heads inside.

Fresh out of the shower and dressed in a pair of sweats, Fred passes Kitt on his way to the kitchen. He gives the place a once over, "The girls did a great job on cleanup," he calls out. He locks up the bungalow, sets the "damned alarm" as Kitt annoyingly refers to it, grabs two wine glasses and Kitt's effervescent Moscato, and sprints to the bedroom. "Sorry about the food-baby incident," he smiles wide. "Let's toast to my stupidity and talk about making a baby." Fred raises his glass.

She declines the glass he offers her. "I can't have this."

"Why not?"

"Because I might be pregnant. I just checked my calendar. I haven't had my period in weeks. I guess secret super-spy drama, and a dying woman's last words on a nightly tumble, aren't compatible with important things like remembering to take birth control."

Fred whoops in celebration.

"You're happy about this?" her hand gently finding her belly.

"Sure. But I'm happier that my detective skills are *awesome*," he singsongs.

Fred and Kitt laugh until she begins sobbing. He pulls her onto his lap. "Kittridge, why are you crying?"

"I told Annie to practice safe sex. All the while I'm knocked up. Again!"

"Oh, Kittridge, don't be so hard on yourself. This is our first knock up."

She stifles her laugh, "Ohhhhh, Fred, this is your first baby," she pauses, "right?"

"Yes, Kittridge, he's my first."

"He?"

"Yeah."

The maybe-expectant-parents have just settled down for a long winter's nap when Kitt's cell rings. She grabs it and shows Fred the display, then answers. "Maura, it's late," she yawns into the phone.

"So are you," her best friend laughs.

"How on earth did you find out?"

"Your detective figured it out and swore my detective to secrecy. Tell Fred it cost me sexually, but we used a condom, so it's all good."

"Hmmmm. Condoms. Never used them myself, but I hear they work. Anyway, if you would have called me five minutes sooner, you could have told me I was pregnant. I had absolutely no idea. It's not definite, by the way, but I'm probably pregnant."

"We're pregnant," Fred corrects.

"Tell Fred I heard that, and I'm gonna go throw up," Maura laughs.

"Me, too," Kitt says before bounding off the bed and scrambling to the bathroom.

"Best detective **ever**!" Fred calls out after her.

THE CARTEL

Carlos Montoya moves his black Lexus toward Cutters. He's been sitting in the damned car all night—he's pissed, he's hungry, and he's up on blow. The hitman followed the orange Jeep from the cemetery, to the bungalow, to the condo building, the night before. Then he watched a buff, but injured dude help a pequeñita puta schlepp her suitcase and duffle inside. They headed up a flight of stairs as Carlos exited his Lexus and moved through the near-empty parking lot. He stopped at the front security door and read the buzzer pad, Monopoli 2A, Bodreau 2B, Sneade 2C, Buck 2D. "Which of these lucky people are you with, pequeñita puta?" Carlos got back into his ride, grabbed his cell to do a little research on the condo residents, only to find that it was, "Fucking dead. Dead. Dead. Dead." He tossed the phone onto the back seat with a snarled threat, "It's only a matter of time before the puta is fucking dead. Dead. Dead. Dead."

Daybreak has come and gone, and it has left in its wake an irritable killer. Carlos tries to stretch out the kinks from being folded in the car all night—quickly finds that his campout isn't the source of his irritability. A thought, more like a dawning of doubt pushes in. "Maybe ..." He gets out of his ride, steps into the tree line, and takes a piss. "I wish I hadn't stepped on that fucking grave, yesterday." He tries to shake the voice of his long, deceased mother from his head…

"Carlos, if you step on a grave you will summon the spirit that lives within and it will haunt you for all of your days."

"Forget the fucking spirit haunting me—I'm a dead man if Uncle Paulo finds out about this." He gets back into the Lexus, snorts a little blow, and simplifies things, "Paulo doesn't find out."

All hell breaks loose.

John has been sitting on the porch for nearly an hour. Correction: John has been freezing his ass off on the porch for nearly an hour. Within a fraction of a second of a warm glow coming from inside the bungalow, he gets off the sofa and gently taps the back door window.

Fred pulls open the door, "Kinda early, John."

"Be thankful I'm not breaking and entering."

Fred steps back to let him through, "Fair enough."

"So, why do you think Tess might be in danger?" he asks pointedly.

Fred reaches into his jeans pocket and hands John the list, then plugs in the coffee percolator.

John skims the paper, "Joy said this to Kitt right before…?"

Fred leans back against the counter and nods.

John reads the note out loud, "John do list pink and white go deep Kitt thank you save Tess Fred message sorry save list Annie system crashed." He tosses the note onto the counter, and goes to the door, "What the hell, Fred?

That's nothing but a bunch of gibberish from a dying woman."

"Your woman. A super-spy. It's a lot more than gibberish," the detective calls after a retreating Special Agent.

Fred crawls back into bed and nestles behind Kitt, resting his cheek on hers. His arm wraps around her waist, and his hand finds her belly. It stays put. She smiles against his cheek, and relaxes into his embrace. The questions that rattled her brain all night are answered with a single touch from the man who loves her.

"Good morning, Fred. Did I hear you talking in the kitchen?"

"Yeah, John stopped by."

She sits up, "You didn't tell him, did you?"

Fred laughs, "No, but he'll eventually find out."

"Fred Chester Serpico, no one else is to know about this until we're sure I'm pregnant, and even then, not until we know what we're doing about it."

Fred bolts up, "What does **that** mean? We're having the baby, right?"

"Of course we are, but this is all so sudden, Fred. We haven't talked about us, and now there's more than us to talk about."

He pulls her back flat on the bed, slides his arm beneath her head, and nestles it in the crook of his elbow, "Kittridge, I'm not going anywhere. I'm where I want to be. Now, if you aren't in for the long haul with me, we will make sure that we put the baby first. You already do that with your girls; we can do the same for our baby."

Kitt runs her fingertips through the scruff on his face and traces his long line dimples, "Fred Serpico, I've been in for the long haul since our faux date." The man she loves laughs big, and offers a typical Fred Serpico response.

"Really, because it took me until our faux, faux, date to go all-in!"

Netti

Special Agent, John Maxwell, has been on leave from FICA since early October. He hasn't been online, hasn't checked his email, or communicated in any way with anyone at the FBI. He knows his protracted absence is pushing things, but he hasn't cared, until now. He needs access to his FICA systems, so he heads to Netti Barn. He could do his work from his home office, but he needs to take back his space. The last time John stepped foot in the barn, he was on a mission to save his daughter, Annie, from the maniac who kidnapped her. In the process, he shot the madman, who moments before had shot Joy Ann Watts—the woman John had been involved with for nearly two decades—the woman he betrayed for most of that time—the woman he still mourns, deeply.

The events of that October day kept John from going back to Netti Barn. Finding out the meaning behind Joy's dying words brings him back.

"John do list pink and white go deep Kitt thank you save Tess Fred message sorry save list Annie system crashed," he practically snarls the words. "Ramblings of a dying woman," he scoffs. "But they're fucking with my head!" He moves about Netti, turning on this, checking on that, and ruminating on the damn list. "Why would Joy spend her last moments on earth muttering nonsense? Wouldn't she express her feelings for Tess, or me?" He makes his way back to the door he just entered, shuts it, and sets security, "Don't need any prying eyes for this work. If there is a message from Joy, it might not be that Tess is in danger, but…"

John sits at his terminal, and flips a switch. A message flashes across his screen, **It's about time, Special Agent Maxwell.** John smiles—the smile is a surprise, the message is a dig, and a trap. "Nice job, Roland. Your little message just sent an auto-reply letting you know that I'm online." John should contact his boss. "Nope." John deletes the message, sets up a secure cyber space, types in Joy's last words and isolates the ones that are a part of his language, (John do list) (go deep) (system crashed). He puts (John do list) aside. His immediate read on that grouping of words is that they have something to do with the alphabetical list he and Joy followed for their annual reunions. His systems can't help with that, but they can take him deep, so John goes deep.

Cutters

Annie helps Mike with his jacket. He's pushed his good arm through one sleeve, but is having trouble swinging the jacket over his brace. She grabs hold of the butter soft leather and flips it up onto his shoulder. In the process she notices a gun in the waistband of his jeans. She raises a brow.

"I can still shoot, Annie. No one is ever fucking with us again."

She nods, and smiles. Sort of.

Officer Michael Monopoli is pumped—he is out of the condo, and he is with his girl, "How about we grab lunch after my ortho appointment? Maybe see if Cluster and Jane are up for it. They're on winter break from the College. What do you think?"

"I think it sounds great, so long as they don't invite my mother. She's on winter break from the College, too."

Mike is still laughing when Annie hops in and closes her door. The officer stops laughing when all hell breaks loose.

Which one of you?

Annie takes a right out of the parking lot onto Slater. Almost immediately, a black Lexus SUV speeds up behind her. "What the hell!" Annie shouts as her eyes bounce back and forth between the windshield and the rearview mirror.

"Don't watch the rearview, Annie, keep looking forward," Mike says as he pulls his mirrored visor down to get a look behind them. The black Lexus is charging forward, then pulling back just shy of hitting the rear bumper. Over and over, the driver charges then retreats.

"Maybe he's in a hurry and wants me to pull over," Annie suggests.

"I don't think so. Just drive the way you are. We'll intersect with Crenshaw in a couple of minutes. If he wants to pass, he can do it then." Mike has been incrementally turning himself in the front seat, despite the impediment of a shoulder brace. He gets a clear view out the back window just as the Lexus speeds up and hits the Jeep's back bumper. "Annie don't speed up. He wants to push you into the four-way intersection up the road. Hold tight to the steering wheel. Keep your speed the same, or slow down. You can do this, Annie." Mike grabs his cell phone and punches 9-1-1. When the dispatcher answers, he says, "Officer Michael Monopoli, badge number

7227, in a Jeep belonging to Annie Mahoney-Maxwell on Slater heading to Crenshaw intersection. Black Lexus SUV in pursuit of Jeep. Trying to run us off..."

"Mike, hold on!" Annie screams.

The Lexus charges the Jeep and makes contact just as a shot rings out.

"Annie, open your eyes. Come on, Sweet Annie. That's my girl. Look at me."

"Which one of you?" the woozy woman asks.

Mike chuckles, "Stay with me, Annie. That's good. Keep your eyes open. I've got to check on the guy in the Lexus."

Within minutes, both vehicles are surrounded by police. Mike is standing at Annie's window trying to keep her awake. He is still holding the gun he fired and is supporting his left elbow in an effort to lessen the pain radiating through his injured shoulder.

Fred and Steve rush to him. Fred takes Mike's weapon, Steve checks Annie, and calls for the arriving EMTs.

Mike starts rambling, a bit in English, a bit in Italian. "Detective Serpico, the uomo in the Lexus is deceduto. Dispatch is still connected to my cell. It's in the veicolo, or what's left of it. You'll want to take it for evidenza, sir."

Fred taps Mike's good shoulder, "I've got it from here, Officer. We're gonna get you two to the hospital, now."

"Yes, sir. Annie could use some tending to."

"You, too, Michael," the detective says. Fred stays with the injured parties until the ambulance takes them to Mayflower-Falls Regional Medical Center.

Steve heads to the Lexus to check out the dead guy.

Netti

John reluctantly answers his phone, "I'm busy, Fred."

"Annie and Mike have been in an accident. Looks like they both have concussions. They are heading to Mayflower-Falls Regional. I need you to get Kittridge and bring her to the hospital. Try to keep her calm, John."

Detective Phelps approaches Detective Serpico with wheels already spinning in his head. Fred reads the signs. "What've you got, Steve?"

"Driver's license lists the dead guy as Caucasian, Frank Russell. He's not Caucasian, and his pinky-ring has the initials CM on it."

"Maybe the initials stand for, Caucasian Male," he laughs.

"Here's something else that'll make you laugh, the address on the registration is from Miami."

"A little far from home," Fred notes.

They both take another look at the guy in the car.

Fred and Steve stay at the crash scene until the non-Caucasian from Miami is zipped into a body bag. When they leave, one detective heads to the hospital, and the other detective heads to the morgue.

Bullet Bungalow

Kitt is shocked to find John at the back door. The shocked part comes from the fact that he is standing on the outside announcing his presence with a knock. She quickly scans her memory. "Nope, John Maxwell has never knocked on my door, not even on the day he moved into my neighborhood when he was twelve."

"We're here!" the woman in the front seat of a station wagon said as it pulled to the curb. Kitt watched from her bedroom window as her new neighbors got out of the car, and started unloading it. When most of the work was done, the boy hopped on his bike and went for a spin around Mayflower. When he came back, he hopped off his bike and let it fall to the ground, even though it had a perfectly good kickstand. Then, he bounded up the Mahoney's backstairs and walked into their house.

Jim Mahoney, Kitt's father, tolerated the intrusion then said, "I think you made a mistake, son, you live next door."

John smirked, "No mistake, sir, just want to introduce myself. I'm John Maxwell."

With that taken care of, the new kid on the block grabbed an apple off the kitchen table and left, Kitt's father calling after him, "Knock next time."

John Maxwell **never** knocked on a Mahoney's door, until today.

"John. This is a shock."

He reaches for her hand. She steps back. He holds tight.

"What's wrong?" she croaks.

"Annie and Mike were in an accident. Fred asked me to take you to the hospital."

She starts to sway and gasp for air. Her hands tingle and feel as though they are no longer attached to her wrists. She feels faint.

John takes hold of her elbow, "Kitt, you're as white as paper. Sit down."

She drops onto the porch sofa, bends over, and puts her head between her knees—her knocking knees.

"Don't move," he says as he runs to get a glass of water and her jacket. "Here, drink this." He sits next to her, drapes the jacket across her shoulders and pats her back. "Let me look at you. Good, your color is coming back."

"I'm better now. We should go."

"After you tell me how far along you are."

Kitt is shocked by his words. There's that word, again, **shocked**. "What is it with men these days? They look at a woman and know she's pregnant. Or maybe it's just detecting and spying men who have this innate ability. Seriously John, how did you know?"

"I've seen the signs with you twice before. Come on, let's go check on our first born."

C-o-n-d-o-m-s

For the fourth time in four months, Annie finds herself in the Emergency department. She lies quietly on a gurney checking her mental acuity by naming the villain responsible for her multiple trips there, "Alden, Alden, Hector, and the asshole in the Lexus."

"Annie," her ambulance and exam room companion calls out to her.

"Yes, Mike."

"What are you doing?"

"Playing a game."

"What game?"

"Six steps to Mahoney Maxwell Mayhem."

Mike holds his laughter, then eggs her on, "How do you play?"

"Well, thus far, I am the only player in this twisted shit fest, so it's rather easy to learn the rules. The object of the game is to figure out who the bad guy is, and why he's pissed at Kitt Mahoney or John Maxwell. Then you try to figure out what the bad guy is going to do to the unsuspecting daughter—that's me.

"In round one, the bad guy was Alden, and he was pissed because Kitt Mahoney had his land, so Alden beat the crap out of the unsuspecting daughter. In round two, the bad guy was Alden again, and this time he was pissed because Kitt Mahoney started dating a cop who figured shit out, so Alden took a shot at the unsuspecting daughter causing her to fall down and go boom. In round three, the bad guy was Hector—actually, the bad guys were Hector and Troy. If you guessed that the lunatic pissed at John Maxwell had two personalities, then good for you—you get bonus points. Anyway, these two-for-one psychos were mad because they didn't get to be the Boy Genius or Boy Geniuses of FICA, so they chloroformed the unsuspecting daughter and kidnapped the shit out of her." Annie stops for a minute, rolls onto her side until she winces in pain and says, "Mike."

"Yes, Annie."

"How much do you want to bet that the bad guy in round four has something to do with a Mahoney or a Maxwell?"

Mike is saved from answering the question by a nurse who comes to take Annie for a CT-scan. "Not a moment too soon," Mike winks at the nurse.

When Annie returns, it is to an empty room. She is told by the ER doc that she has a concussion, the second in that many months, and will be spending a few days as an inpatient. Her wrist is ace bandaged and resting in a sling, the result of the pounding it took from holding the steering wheel while the Jeep was repeatedly hit from behind. She takes the news all in stride, then asks about Mike.

The doctor shrugs, the nurse smiles, "He's having tests. Before he left he said to tell you that there's no way this doesn't have something to do with a Mahoney or a Maxwell. He said you'd understand."

Annie smirks, "Oh, believe you me, I understand."

Fred is waiting at the sliding glass doors when John and Kitt arrive at the hospital. There is a noticeable pause in John's step before he enters. Kitt notes that it's the first time he's been at the Regional Center since Joy died there. She pretends that she doesn't notice his pause.

The three visitors are led to Annie's holding room by a nurse whose name Kitt should remember. After all, she's seen her quite a bit lately, but then again, each time they'd met, Kitt had been on the receiving end of a bump upside her head. She simply smiles, a knowing sort of smile, and moves on. The visitors are deposited at Annie's room, and even though her daughter looks none the worse for wear, Kitt loses it when she sees her on the stretcher. She grabs hold of Annie as though only one of them can board a lifeboat off the Titanic.

"Geez, Mom, you weren't this emotional after Alden or Hector. What's crawled up your emotional butt?" Annie scoffs.

No one responds.

Annie looks back and forth. The guilty parties nervously avoid her stare. John, the well-established traitor steps back. "This doesn't concern me," he says.

Annie looks back and forth between Fred Serpico and Kittridge Mahoney. The goofball standing next to the fidgeting woman suddenly sports the strangest smile anyone has ever seen on a *living* human being. Kitt wants to smack the smile off him, which is perplexing because she usually loves his smile—not this smile, mind you. It's at that point that the goofball standing next to Creepy Smiling Man decides to move her hand to her abdomen.

The pit bull on the stretcher attacks, "No way. Oh. My. God. No way. This question might be the result of my being concussed repeatedly, but are you pregnant, Mother? Before you answer that question, I need to throw something out there: c-o-n-d-o-m-s."

Mike, who is being wheeled into the holding room looks at the snarling mutt and asks, "Annie, why are you spelling? And why are you spelling the word condoms?"

Bullet Bungalow
John calls Tess and Callie from the hospital and tells them about the accident and instructs them to stay in the bungalow with the security engaged. Fred calls Officer Grant Speil and tells him to watch the bungalow until they all get

home. He is emphatic, "No one goes in, no one goes out, Speil."

After Annie and Mike are settled in their rooms, Kitt, John, and Fred put the emergency part of the day behind them and head to the bungalow to hang out with the doppelgangers. Fred and Kitt arrive home first, followed immediately by John. Two of the three stopped on the way for a pregnancy test, the other one stopped for a couple of pizzas. The girls squeal their delight that the pizzas came from their favorite place, The Pizza Crust. It should be noted that they squealed their delight in unison. "Best sound ever," the adults say in unison. The teens nudge each other, and head to the living room for a coffee table picnic.

Since Kitt is having trouble with the sight and smell of the pizza, she eagerly watches them leave, then tells Fred and John to eat their pootieball (sausage) pizza outside.

"A bit cold outside, Kittridge."

"Wear a coat, Fred."

"It's gonna be a long nine months," he scoffs.

John smirks.

Kitt points to the door, "Don't let it hit…"

Fred laughs big.

They spoon all night.

"I'm glad Kitt kicked us out of the house."

"A fan of frozen pootieballs, are you, John?"

"I did a little cyber investigating, today."

"Didn't know you were back to work."

"I'm not. I needed to access my systems." John puts his half-eaten slice down and takes a sip of his soda, "The list started bothering me. It's probably gibberish, but Joy could have said so many other things at the time of her death. I decided to work the list by addressing the cyber related things she said. You know, (go deep) (system crashed)."

"And?"

"I think Joy **was** sending a message."

The men move to the warmth of John's SUV—the men move out of earshot of Kitt.

"Spill it, John."

"I went deep. I let it be known that I was in cyberland. Then I called a few cyber agents who worked the Hector case to see where they've been assigned. They haven't been reassigned. They are still focused on Hector."

"Hector is dead. I know this because I saw you shoot the 'fucker'. Maybe the Feds should get with the program," Fred says pointedly.

John sends Fred a "shut up" look.

Fred shuts up.

"The death of Hector has caused some nationwide unrest amongst the drug lords. Without pre-raid warnings from the cyber-drug-savior, the cartels are behind the eight-ball again. The syndicates have banded together and waged all-out war on the DEA. Two agents were killed, execution style, in Greenwich Village the other night." John gives Fred a minute to process what this means for his DEA ex-wife, Special Agent, Veronica Shields, then continues, "As far as (Annie system crashed) is concerned, I'm not sure about the Annie part, but Joy's system was crashed."

Fred shrugs, "Wouldn't it be standard operating procedure for FICA to crash the computer system of a deceased super-spy?"

"Yes, Fred, FICA would do that **after** the super-spy becomes deceased. Joy's system was crashed **before** she died, and it was crashed by Joy."

"You're sure?"

"I'm sure."

Steve knocks on John's window and laughs when the super-spy and super-detective jump. John opens his window. "I should take your head off, Phelps."

"Yeah, but then you two wouldn't know what I know."

John flips open the locks, "Get in."

Steve hands Fred a preliminary Medical Examiner's report with a fingerprint analysis attached, "Let me recap it for you. The dead dude in the Lexus is not Caucasian Frank Russell. He is Hispanic Carlos Montoya. His uncle is Paulo Montoya, the most successful drug lord on the eastern corridor. Now, one might ask what Carlos Montoya, a drug lord's contract killer, is doing in little old Mayflower? One might also ask why this contract killer tried to run a Federal Agent's daughter and an MFPD officer off the road. It's anyone's guess, and I suggest we start guessing."

Manhattan
DEA Special Agent, Veronica Shields, reads an email marked Urgent. One thing in the email makes her very happy: Carlos Montoya, aka Frank Russell, is dead. It's the other thing that makes her very unhappy: Detective Fred Serpico, aka her ex-husband, was at the scene of death.

"What the hell?"

Bullet Bungalow
Fred slips into bed, trying not to wake Kitt. She watches through pretend sleeping eyes as he lays his head on his pillow, only to realize that something shares the resting space. "The pregnancy test," he whispers to whomever happens to be listening—Kitt happens to be

listening. He tries to read the results in the very dark room, and starts to get out of bed.

"Go to sleep, Daddy, you're going to need your rest," she whispers.

He pulls her into his spoon, "I'm happy, Kittridge."

"Me, too, Fred."

"Just one thing."

"And that would be?"

"You peed on a stick and put it on my pillow. Switch pillows," he laughs.

He pulls her tight. They spoon all night.

THE CARTEL

Paulo Montoya snorts from one of ten pave diamond encrusted coke spoons that are spread across his desk. In between snorts he rages about Carlos. "That stupido nephew of mine is dead, stupido and dead. If that crazy muthafucka wasn't laying his ass in a morgue, I'd fuck him up real good, put a bullet through his head, and send his ass to a morgue!"

Marco Martinez, the person who informed Paulo Montoya about Carlos is knee deep in the dead fucker's shit, and on the receiving end of Paulo's rage.

"I gave my no-good nephew one damn job, go to fucking Mayflower and grab the kid. That's it. Did I tell him to do anything to anyone else? NO! He almost killed my whole fucking plan. I want the kid, Marco. I need the kid for my plan to work." Paulo opens his desk drawer and pulls a satchel from inside. He grabs several banded stacks of bills, "You go, Marco. Get Tess Maxwell. Bring her here, alive. Whatever you do, don't lay a finger on her cyber bitch sister. I'll get her when the time is right. Mess this up, Marco, you're dead." Paulo leans over his desk and spoons, all night.

Keep the kids out of the cemetery.

Fred enters the kitchen and finds Tess and Kitt having words.

"Nothing happened, I was just freaked out," Tess demands.

"Something happened, Tess. We don't know what, but something freaked you out."

"I looked around, Mom. No one was there."

"You didn't look behind every monument or tree. There could have been someone there. Look, I'm not saying you can't go to the cemetery, I just don't want you going alone anymore."

"Fine!" Tess shouts as she runs from the room and up the stairs.

Fred pours himself some coffee and leans back against the counter, "Do I want to know?"

"Annie drove through the cemetery the other day to see if Tess was there and if she wanted a ride home. Annie said that when she started driving toward Tess, she bolted down the hill where Joy's grave is and threw herself into the Jeep. Annie said that Tess was freaked out because she was sure someone was watching her. When they got home, Tess was visibly upset. I told her that I don't want her going to the cemetery alone, anymore. That's when you walked in."

Fred finishes his coffee and puts his mug into the dishwasher, "Kittridge, when did you say the freak out happened?"

"I didn't say, Fred."

"Right. So, Kittridge, when did the freak out happen?"

"Tuesday, around dinnertime." Fred kisses Kitt as she heads to her home office.

"Hey, Kittridge, keep the kids out of the cemetery. Well, that's a sentence I never thought I'd say."

"Goodbye, Fred."

Netti

Fred calls John from his truck, "Steve and I are on our way." When the detectives arrive, they find the farmhouse back door open.

"No need for the B&E, today," John calls out.

The detectives find him in his version of a family room—it's really a man's room. A roaring fire has taken hold in a century-old fieldstone fireplace that's set between two forest green painted walls. Around the room there are floor to ceiling paneled sections with built-in bookcases. Overstuffed, oxblood leather club chairs and ottomans sit on either side of the fireplace, and a matching couch fills the rest of the space. One chair is clearly used more than the other and is currently being used by the man of the house. He's pulled a heavy wood coffee table in front of him, the top of which is covered with computer printouts and sheets of handwritten notes.

Fred points to the papers, "What's all that?"

"Annie's research on Hector. I was just about to burn it, but something stopped me. When Annie gets out of the hospital, I'll ask her if she wants it. Maybe there's something in her research that might help us with this case. It's a long shot, but…"

Fred stares hard at John.

"What?"

"You've been out of it for a while, so you don't know. Annie hasn't touched a computer since that night."

A heavy silence settles. "Really?"

"Not once," Fred confirms.

"What about school, Fred. She doesn't use her computer for school?"

"Annie took a leave of absence this semester. She'll still graduate in May, though." Fred waits while John gathers his thoughts and the papers from the table, and stacks them onto the floor. He gives John another minute, then claps his hands signaling that he's ready to begin, "I've got something. Tuesday afternoon Tess went to the cemetery, as she does most days. Annie drove through the cemetery to see if Tess was there and if she wanted a ride home, as she does most days. When Tess saw Annie coming toward her, she bolted from the bench at Joy's grave, ran down the hill, and threw herself into the Jeep. Tess told Annie that she was sure someone was watching her. Annie told Kittridge that she's never seen Tess so freaked out. This morning, after a heated exchange, Kittridge told Tess that she isn't allowed to go to the cemetery alone."

"Good," John grunts.

"Like I said, this happened Tuesday around dinnertime. The next morning Annie and Mike were almost killed by a hitman from Miami. Coincidence?"

"No such thing as coincidence, Fred," Detective Phelps adds his two cents.

Detective Serpico nods, "I asked Mike if he's seen anything suspicious around Cutters lately. He said he hasn't been out much, but he did see a black Lexus in the parking lot Tuesday night when Annie came by with her suitcase and duffle. The driver of that Lexus was probably Carlos Montoya. Mike is convinced that the driver was trying to run them into the intersection of Slater and Crenshaw."

"Interesting way for a hit to go down," Detective Phelps tosses in another two cents.

Fred nods, "Let's break this down. Tuesday afternoon, Tess was freaked out because she thought someone was watching her at a cemetery that she goes to most every day. Tuesday night, Mike saw a black Lexus at Cutters at the same time Annie was arriving for the night. Wednesday morning, a professional hitman, behind the wheel of a black Lexus, tried to kill Annie and Mike. Annie was most likely the target of the attempted hit. The first thing a professional hitman is gonna know is the address of his mark. In this case, it's the same address for both girls. He follows one of the girls to the bungalow, he automatically has the other girl under surveillance."

"But Annie has been staying at Mike's, and that's where the hitman got to her," Steve interjects.

"So let's break this down even further. Montoya had been watching the girls, or one of the girls. He was at the cemetery on Tuesday when Tess was there. Annie showed up and rescued Tess. Montoya followed Annie and Tess to the bungalow. He followed Annie to Mike's. The next morning, he tried to kill Annie. He probably stayed near Cutters all night and took the first opportunity he got to make the hit. The way I run this—Montoya was at the cemetery to take Tess. Annie showed up and ruined his plans. He knew he couldn't get Tess with Annie around. Solution: take out Annie, then take Tess." Fred gets up from his seat and looks at the four corners of the room, "Where are the goddamn windows, John?"

"In the living room, the kitchen, and the bedrooms. Why?"

Steve answers John's question, "Fred needs to look out a window when he's onto something. It's his way of processing."

Fred sprints out of the room and returns several minutes later, "What if Joy knew both girls were in danger? When Joy said, (save list Annie system crashed), maybe the word list wasn't a word, maybe it was an intake of breath or something. Joy already said the word list, (John do list) so why repeat it? If we take out the word list, we end up with (save Annie system crashed)."

Steve gets up and starts pacing.

John furrows and asks Fred, "What is he doing?"

"Pacing. He paces when he organizes the elements of a case. When he's done, he's gonna ramble the facts. It's worth the pacing."

"Recap," Steve corrects.

"Right," Fred laughs.

John shakes his head, "You guys are freaks."

As soon as John's proclamation is finished, Steve starts his ramble. "Joy is shot. While she is dying, she utters her final words. We decided that they are clues, and started pulling threads. Joy said to (go deep). John took a dive and found out that the FBI is still working the Hector case. But Hector is dead—shot by our very own John Maxwell. The reason the Feds are still working the Hector case is because the death of the cyber-drug-savior has pissed off the drug syndicates. They wage war on the DEA, and kill two agents. **All of that makes sense**. A contract killer from Miami comes to Mayflower. He doesn't try to kill John Maxwell—the guy who killed Hector—the cyber-drug-savior—who no longer saves millions for the cartels. Instead, the Miami hitman tries to take Tess—he fails—he tries to kill Annie—he fails. **None of that makes sense**. Loop back to Joy's dying words. They might be clues for us to follow—but they feel more like directives, (save Tess) and (save Annie). If it is a mandate, that's some serious shit for a dying woman. Did she know something? Did she have a premonition? Joy crashed her system, **before** she died. Did she think she was gonna die? Was she planning to go off the grid? She was pissed at John. She was pissed at FICA. Did she decide to walk away from everything?"

Fred pipes in, "Kittridge said that Joy wanted to meet Tess. I don't think she'd meet Tess, and then leave Tess."

John pushes in. "There's no way Joy would meet her daughter and then leave her. She decided a long time ago that meeting Tess and working for FICA were mutually exclusive. Maybe on the last night of her life, Joy decided to leave the Agency for Tess."

Fred gets up to look out a window and remembers there are none, "I have two things to say. First, this room is a fucking cave and it's not fit for man nor beast. Second, maybe Joy was gonna go off the grid, or maybe she was gonna leave FICA so she could meet Tess, OR maybe the almighty DOA was finally unmasked."

"Joy would have crashed her system if **that** happened," John says with finality.

THE CARTEL

Marco Martinez arrives at Logan International Airport high on coke and life. It has been years since Paulo Montoya sent his right-hand-man on a job—years since Marco was out from under his boss' watchful eye. When Marco first started working for the syndicates, he was a freelance contract killer, a good, clean, efficient assassin who liked his blow, living low, and traveling from one dead body to the next. It didn't matter what Marco liked. Within a matter of months of making a name for himself, traveling from coast to coast, and corpse to corpse, Mr. Montoya came knocking on the hitman's door. Sort of.

Marco entered his ground-level apartment through a garden-patio slider. He knew the instant he stepped inside that he wasn't alone. He made the slightest move toward his piece…
    "Don't fucking think about it."
    Though he'd only worked for the Miami boss a handful of times, he knew who was in his place, and why he'd come to L.A.
    "Sit down, Marco."
    The ruthless killer did as he was told.

"You work for me, now." Paulo sneered with his trademark "don't fuck with me" smile on his pockmarked face, and 9mm Luger in his hand.

Marco flew out of L.A. that night, and has been by Paulo Montoya's side ever since. He works exclusively on the inside—he hates the business end of the syndicate, but Marco likes living, so Marco does the business end.

Today, the crime lord wants to use Marco as a contract kidnapper, and Marco is happy to oblige. "Carlos fucked up. Marco lucks out," he says to his shot of tequila. The career criminal is waiting in an airport lounge for Montoya's Boston people to deliver weapons and wheels. While he waits, he enjoys some booze and the bevy of broads passing by on the concourse. Blonde, brunette, tall, short, big tits, little tits— Marco loves them all. Lost in his lust fest, he almost misses a Halle Berry lookalike on stilts. The statuesque woman has black shorn hair, light eyes, a face of perfection, and a body made for pounding. "Black Beauty, come this way," Marco growls.

The woman, who is flanked on either side by men, heads in his direction. She glances into the bar's front window as she moves past. Marco chokes on the shot he just pulled. "Well, well, Black Beauty, a minute ago I wanted to screw you until you begged for release. Now I want to make you beg for your life." The very excited Marco raises his empty shot glass toward the bartender, grabs his cell, and punches in his boss' number, "Mr. Montoya, Veronica Shields is in town." Marco hops from the barstool, drains his shot, throws a $100 bill onto the bar, and sprints outside. He flags a cab and barks instructions, "Follow the black Discovery with tinted windows." He makes a call, "Change of plans. Meet me outside the DEA building in Boston. Someone's in town, and that's where she'll be heading."

The L-Ride cab carrying Marco Martinez follows the Discovery carrying DEA Special Agent, Veronica Shields, through the trafficked streets of Beantown. The SUV pulls into an underground parking facility at the DEA building, the cab pulls to a stop a block away. Marco gets out, tosses the driver a $100 bill for a $30 fare, "Keep the change, you filthy animal," he laughs a cokehead's laugh.

The cabbie does not laugh. He stuffs the hundred into the company cashbox, and documents the tip onto this fare log. He is still at the curb when a black Escalade pulls to a stop across from the Federal building.

Marco sprints across the street and gets in the back of the Escalade. There are two goons in the front, and on the seat next to Marco is a duffle full of guns and ammunition. Marco rummages through, pulls out a handgun and slips it into the waistband of his jeans, pulls another and straps it to his ankle. He notices driver goon watching him in the rearview mirror. Before the goon blinks an eye, he feels Marco's gun pressed to his temple.

"Don't ever look at me. Where's the blow?"

Passenger goon hands it off without making eye contact. Marco leans back and gets high on coke and life.

Turner Blakely is in his cab across the street from the black Escalade. He knows that the guys inside are bad news, and that, "Whoever's in the Discovery is in trouble." Turner pulls a notebook from his backpack, writes down the license plate number of the Escalade, and pulls out into bumper to bumper traffic.

Your recent flogging.

Callie, Tess, and Kitt enter Annie's hospital room early afternoon. The mother of the three girls is carrying a bouquet of pink balloons for Annie, and a bouquet of blue balloons for Mike. Annie raises a quizzical brow. The mother plays dumb because in this case she is. Ignorance may be bliss, but in this case, it's also temporary.

"Oh, God, it's twins," Annie groans.

"What's twins?" the younger girls ask.

Kitt grabs hold of the runaway conversation, the one that is barreling toward the cliff, "Ignore Annie, she's suffering a concussion. She doesn't know what she's saying."

Annie cracks up laughing and is momentarily unable to stop herself.

"See," Kitt says to Callie and Tess, "She's delusional."

When Annie has laughed herself sore, she calls Mike and asks if he's up for visitors. He is, so she pawns off her sisters. "Mike had surgery yesterday, so behave," Annie calls after the doppelgangers, seconds before her face gets all serious and shit.

Kitt slogs into what may be rising waters. "Annie, has something changed with your health status?"

"No."

"Is Mike going to be okay?"

"The doctors think so, but he reinjured his shoulder, so it's going to set him back. He's Mike though, he just rolls with the punches. I like that about him," she smiles wide.

"I like that about him, too," Kitt matches her daughter's smile.

A heavy silence fills the room. It's a couple of minutes before Annie speaks, "Mom, there's something I think I want you to do for me."

"You think, but you aren't sure?"

"I keep going back and forth—it's a big decision."

Kitt waits. Given that she is with this particular daughter, the one who usually pushes into every situation, Kitt finds the wait troublesome. "Annie…"

"Will you bring my computer the next time you visit?" she blurts out.

"Really? That's it? That's the big decision?" The look on Annie's face lets the mother know that she trivialized something very big. Kitt goes into mom-mode, and begins soothing and atoning, "Oh, I'm sorry, Annie. I guess in the scheme of things, you know, car accidents, concussions, and surgeries, I expected something else. Is there any specific reason why you want your computer?"

"Not sure. I just know that I need to go online. It's time."

Netti

The farmhouse has become command central for the decoding of Joy's final words. Fred agrees to work the case from Netti, so long as they work in a room with windows. They settle on the kitchen, a huge room with a farmer's table and eight chairs, a fireplace with two club chairs on either side, and all the necessities of a well-necessitated kitchen. The men choose their seats: Fred's has a window view, Steve has pulled over a second chair to put his feet upon, and John has parked his ass on a kitchen counter; with a clap of Fred's hands they get started.

"Let's recap. We all agree that (John do list) is most likely about the ABC Love Tours—but Joy could have made other lists," he eyes John.

The Special Agent shakes his head, "After running that possibility, I'm sure she was referring to our reunion list. When Joy worked, she used white boards that she could erase. She never left a trace of anything behind; more important, there wasn't any ambiguity in the way Joy communicated. (John do list). That is a directive and it is precise. Joy wanted me to focus on this particular clue." He tosses two copies of the list onto the table.

Fred scans it. His eyes stop when he sees the city of Seattle. "Well, it looks like we just got our first thread to pull." So Fred and John start pulling.

Steve gets up and starts pacing through the farmhouse, it takes several minutes for him to light again. "Are you two seriously thinking that (John do list) was Joy's way of telling us to find Seattle, think Veronica, think DEA, think Hector—because we need to (save Tess) and (save Annie)?"

"Yes." Fred and John agree in unison.

"And you think we should disregard the other cities on the reunion list?"

"Yes!" Fred and John shout in…

"If that's the case, and this is about DEA Special Agent, Veronica Shields, maybe Fred should reach out to his ex-wife."

John smirks.

Fred shakes his head, "Let's put **that** on the backburner. Next up, (pink and white). This has got to be about that godawful pink and white chevron wallpaper in Tess' bedroom. Joy spent her last night alive in that room, and that experience alone **had** to have messed with her head, but it might be something more than that…"

"That's a damn shame," Steve interrupts.

"That she died, or that she died after being subjected to that damned room?"

John smirks.

Steve shakes his head, "Better be careful, Fred, or God just might smite you."

"He smites me every time I have to go near that damned room."

"Silver lining, Fred, you weren't the one who had to hang the paper."

Fred laughs. "Should have known it was you, John. Okay, maybe the (pink and white) is a one-off, or maybe it means something. I don't think we have enough to work with, so why don't we come back to this later? It might have a connection to one of the other clues."

John jumps in. "As far as (go deep) is concerned, I know I found something already, but cyberland presents near endless possibilities. You know, Fred, we could really use Annie on this. She's like Joy in the deep. She's aggressive, and she's a huntress. If there's something to be found, Annie is our best asset."

"I don't disagree, John, but there are two problems with that. One, Annie isn't working with computers right now. Two, Kittridge would do serious damage to me if I got Annie into any of this. I believe your recent flogging proves that point."

"Yeup. Then I guess we're at (Kitt thank you save Tess). I was thinking, if we divide this into two parts, we get (Kitt thank you) and (save Tess)…"

"That's Fred's line of thinking, too," Steve tosses in. "I don't disagree, but I've been thinking about this, a lot. Joy was critically wounded when she rambled all of this." He stops and gives his partner a good long look, "For the record, Detective Serpico, what Joy Ann Watts did that day can be described as rambling."

Fred laughs. "Please continue, Detective Phelps."

"Joy took a bullet to the back. She had to have known she was dying. Instead of going all nostalgic or philosophical, she tossed out a bunch of clues—to a woman she had a complicated relationship with—the woman she regarded as being Tess' mother. Think back to when we were at the bungalow and the shit was hitting the fan about John being a spy, things got really tense when Kitt learned that Joy had masqueraded as Fee Peterson. Kitt blew up, said a few choice words, and stormed out of the bungalow."

"Fee Peterson!" **Kitt screamed,** "The intern who worked with John at Netti Barn when the girls and I first moved to the farmhouse? The intern who **never** seemed to be at Netti when I was around? The intern who my kids thought hung the moon? The intern who played with them, read stories to them, and bandaged their boo-boos when I was at work?" **Kitt turned to** the man who betrayed her like no other. "How could you? You knew I didn't want Joy or Fee or DOA or whoever the hell she is, anywhere near Annie, Callie, or Tess. Oh. My. God. Tess. You let Joy be with Tess, to hold and cuddle Tess? Was that fun for you, John? And **you**," Kitt turned back to Joy, "you didn't want that sweet baby. You gave her up for a job. A job that lists you as DOA. If I could get my hands on a gun right now, you would be a different kind of D.O.A., and so would you, John." Kitt stormed out onto the back porch.

"When she came back, Joy walked to Kitt, looked her in the eye and said, 'Kitt, I should start by thanking you. I am deeply indebted to you for being a mother to Tess—for being her mother'. That was some heavy shit. Now jump ahead to (Kitt thank you save Tess) and combo this up. You could get, (Kitt thank you), that's a sentimental statement; you could also get, (you save Tess), that's a desperate plea."

"Desperate plea..." Fred gets up and looks out the kitchen window at Netti Barn. "Desperate plea..."

John pushes in, "Fred. Are you processing, or..."

He talks to the men over his shoulder, "I already told you that Joy grabbed hold of my arm when John and I were scrambling out of Bullet Bungalow. She said, 'Fred, I need to tell...' Her look, her hold on my arm, her desperate plea. I made the assumption that she needed to tell ME something, but that doesn't have to be the case. I only knew Joy a handful of hours. If she had something of urgency, something of significance to tell someone, why was I that someone?"

Steve is up pacing, "Let's figure out why Joy approached Fred, and not John." He goes for a pace through the farmhouse. "If she wanted to say something about crashing her system, it's most likely she would have told John. No matter how much bad blood there was between them, they were both Feds, working in the same division, for the same boss. Seems like a straight line to me—Joy has something work related to say, she's gonna say it to the asshole she works with," he laughs.

"Fuck you, Phelps."

"So, maybe Joy was gonna tell Fred something about Tess, or ask him to give her a message. You said Joy was the last one to get to the kitchen because she came from Tess' room. Maybe something happened while Joy was up there that caused her to crash her system, and she was going to tell Fred about it..."

Fred jumps in, "Or, maybe something happened in Tess' room, and she left me some sort of message. Maybe that's how we connect to (pink and white). Maybe there's a clue in Tess' room." Fred let's his words hang for a minute then adds, "Well, my night just hit the shits. I have to call my ex-wife, **and** I need to spend time in the Devil's waiting room."

Steve and John laugh.

Fred does not.

THE CARTEL

The goons debate about who is going to wake Marco. Passenger goon decides for himself. He pushes a control button and lowers the window nearest to Marco's head. A frigid blast of cold air assaults the Floridian. He opens his eyes, his gun already trained on driver goon. "You have a death wish?" Driver goon ignores him and pulls the Escalade into traffic a few cars behind the Discovery.

"She's on the move," driver goon grunts.

The Discovery and the Escalade inch along the streets of Boston, and as soon as they merge onto I-93N, the cartel kidnapper knows they are going to Mayflower. He calls his boss. "Looks like DEA Shields is heading to Mayflower. Maybe she's in town to get confirmation that Carlos is dead. She seems a bit high on the DEA food chain to be checking this out, but..."

"Follow her. Then get the kid."

A yellow L-Ride cab tracks the two car caravan out of Boston towards all points north. The creeping cabbie, Turner Blakely, has no idea where the Discovery and the Escalade are heading. More to the point, he has no fucking idea why he is following them. "You're a journalism major, not an investigative reporter," Turner admonishes himself, before pressing the accelerator so he doesn't lose sight of the vehicles.

Skipping beats.

The men have been working all day on Joy's final words and want a few more hours at it. Fred does a calzone, wings, and a six pack of Sam Adams run while John and Steve review Annie's papers. The guys have no sooner pulled a sip, and taken their first bite, when headlights cut across the living room. John heads to the front door and shares a few words with whomever has arrived. Fred and Steve hear the sounds of muffled voices—John's and a woman's.

"Well this is interesting," they laugh.

The front door closes and John calls out, "Fred, your wife is here."

Fred is expecting to see Kitt when he approaches the living room—he gets Veronica Shields, instead. For the first time in more than a year, Fred Serpico is in the same room with the woman he fell in love with – the woman he married while still in college – the woman he spent more than a decade with – the woman who chose her career over him. The woman who just made his heart skip a beat. "Roni."

"Serp."

After those two words, there is nothing. No sound. No movement. No life sustaining breathing. Steve cracks under the pressure.

"Well, now that these two have been introduced, Special Agent Shields, I'm…"

"I know who you are, Detective Phelps. It's nice to meet you," Veronica crosses the room and shakes Steve's hand.

Steve's heart skips a beat.

Roni turns to John, "I'm sorry I was unable to attend Joy's services. I sent a note; I hope you received it."

John nods.

"I wanted to let you know that Joy kept in touch with me through the years. I know I'm confessing to breaking protocol, but I thought you'd appreciate knowing she wasn't a ghost to everyone."

"It did help. Thank you, Roni." If John still had a working heart, it would have skipped a beat.

Roni insists that the men finish their meals. John and Steve empty their plates—Fred doesn't eat a thing. He leaves the kitchen and stands in front of the living room bay window, arms folded across his chest, feet spread wide, and legs locked tight.

"Good to know some things never change," Roni says from behind him.

"Yeah, me and a window," Fred turns and leans against the cold glass, arms still folded tight. "Are you here because of Montoya?"

"Yes."

"You work the West Coast. You got it in our divorce settlement, remember? Montoya is East Coast, so why are you here, Roni?"

"Because you're here, Serp."

"Water over the dam, or under the bridge, or wherever the hell it goes, Roni." Fred pushes off of the window, and walks past his ex-wife. He brings a whole lot of tension back into the kitchen.

His partner helps him out. "Two detectives, a super-spy, and a DEA agent walk into a farmhouse kitchen: just an ordinary night in the seaside village of Mayflower." He gets the chuckle he hoped for.

Roni Shields crashed the party, so she explains why, "Yesterday, I received an email informing me that Carlos Montoya, contract killer and nephew of Paulo Montoya, was dead. I found that bit of news rather delightful. Then I learned that Carlos died in Mayflower, and one of the detectives involved in the case is my ex-husband, Fred Serpico. I found that bit of news rather disturbing. Questions started popping left and right. First pop: what was a career criminal, a contract killer no less, from Miami doing in Mayflower? Then I remembered that 'two detectives and a super-spy' took down the notorious Hector, and they all live in Mayflower. Seeing as there is major blowback from drug syndicates across the country because their cyber-drug-savior is dead, I thought maybe there was a hit put out on one of you three. I'm here to find out what's going on, gentlemen, so let's begin."

John and Steve are suddenly rendered mute. They leave Fred out on his own. He's pissed at just about everything and comes loaded for bear, "I'm sure you've read all the reports on the kidnapping of Annie Mahoney-Maxwell and the killing of Joy Ann Watts, aka DOA."

Roni nods.

"And in spite of your previous denials, you know, and have always known—that John Maxwell and Joy Ann Watts are, or were, undercover agents for FICA."

Roni shifts in her seat and nods.

"And you know that Hector spent years trying to unmask the preeminent huntress and preeminent defender of FICA because as you say, 'you broke protocol' by having a friendship with Joy, and she probably confided that."

Roni nods.

"See Roni, no intake of breath. That's how I know you're telling the truth this time," Fred jabs and holds her glare.

"Having fun, Serp?"

"A little bit," he nods. After a few seconds he claps his hands and moves on, "Before Hector shot Joy from the loft window of Netti Barn, he had his gun trained on Kittridge Mahoney, the mother of kidnap victim Annie

Mahoney-Maxwell. As best we can tell, Joy saw a flash when Hector sighted his rifle, and she tackled Kittridge—subsequently taking a bullet to the back. As Joy lay dying, she spoke a series of words. Over time, those words started bothering Kittridge, so she wrote them down and shared them with me. At first, I thought the words were the ramblings of a dying woman, but…"

Roni interrupts her ex-husband, "But you processed and came up with something."

"Yeah. And I don't like being interrupted."

Roni laughs, "I remember."

He continues. "I recently shared the list with Steve and John. The three of us are convinced that Joy's dying words are clues, and if we follow them, we will (save Tess), John's daughter with Joy, and (save Annie), John's daughter with Kittridge. We had just started decoding Joy's words, when Carlos Montoya showed up in Mayflower and attempted to kill Annie and Mike Monopoli, an MFPD officer. Annie lives with her mother, but recently began spending time at Officer Monopoli's place. We think Montoya followed Annie from the cemetery where Joy is buried, to the Mahoney home, to Monopoli's condo on Tuesday evening. We also think that Montoya planned on taking Tess Maxwell from the cemetery, Tuesday afternoon. If that's the case, the kidnapping was prevented by Annie when she showed up to give her sister a ride home."

Roni jumps in. "If Joy's message is a directive to (save Tess) and (save Annie), the primary question for me is: why would Montoya want these two girls? It sounds like you guys think he wants one dead and the other kidnapped—why? If the Montoya cartel wants retribution for Hector's death, why not kill Maxwell since he's the one who shot the cyber-drug-savior? And if that doesn't satisfy the drug syndicates, then they could take out all three of you. The organizations have a legitimate bitch with you guys, not the girls."

"Valid questions. So far, there's been no move against any of us, and no move has been made against Callie, John's third daughter. If all three girls were targeted I'd think this was retaliation against John for killing Hector. But the two girls targeted are the same two girls that a dying Joy thought needed saving. What we know for sure is this, Tess has been sitting at her mother's grave for months with no issues. Tuesday, she was freaked out by the feeling that someone was watching her. On Wednesday, Annie and Mike were practically forced off the road into an intersection by a Lexus driven by a contract killer. If Mike hadn't been in Annie's Jeep, and shot out the front window of the Lexus, killing the driver, Annie would be dead. Another thing, Roni, a contract killer of a drug lord chose to use a Lexus to kill his mark? I believe the standard operating procedure is a bullet to the head."

Roni shifts uncomfortably in her seat.

Fred notices, but continues, "Running a mark off the road with an innocent ride-along, a cop no less, is rather sloppy."

"Or recklessly impulsive. Carlos Montoya was nuts—certifiable. Paulo Montoya usually kept Carlos on a tight leash. I'm surprised that the drug lord turned him loose on this seaside village. This job is more suited to Paulo's business manager and former hitman, Marco Martinez."

"Should we expect a visit from Mr. Martinez?" Steve asks.

"You better hope not, Detective Phelps, Marco Martinez **never** misses his mark."

THE CARTEL

The goons and the kidnapper drive past a pale yellow, two-story farmhouse just as Black Beauty steps through the front door. Her muscle remains outside: one bodyguard stays in the Discovery, one stands at the rear bumper. Marco sneers at the DEA Special Agent. "You lucked out in Greenwich, Special Agent Shields, but luck won't be on your side the next time a Montoya employee pays a call. Especially if I'm the one knocking on your fucking door," Marco laughs.

Driver goon travels the length of Farm Road Low, and through the main streets of Mayflower before heading back. He pulls the Escalade off to the side of the road a quarter mile shy of the farmhouse. Marco looks at the array of vehicles parked on the driveway. "A black Discovery. A black F-150. A black BMW. A black Land Rover. What is she at, a convention of black rides?" Marco laughs. "Pull the Escalade in, they probably won't even notice us."

Driver goon starts the engine. Marco points his gun at the driver's head, "Stupido, turn it off." The cartel businessman stretches out across the back, presses against the door, and pulls his legs up onto the seat. He trains his eyes on the driveway, until he is distracted by approaching headlights that cut a path across a yellow car that's pulled off to the side of the road beyond the farmhouse. "I think we were followed." He taps passenger goon on the shoulder, "Check out the car up there. If it's a yellow cab, it's probably the one I took from the airport. Take care of whoever's in it, and be back before we leave, or find your own way back to Boston."

Turner Blakely has just put his notebook into his backpack when there is a tap on the driver's side window. The young cabbie knows he's a dead man one second before he becomes a dead man.

Halilue Berryah.

Annie sneaks down to Mike's hospital room after lights out. He is asleep when she sits next to his bed. He wakes at the touch of her hand on his.

"Annie, are you alright? Shouldn't you be in bed?"

"I was missing you."

Mike runs his fingertips across Annie's cheek. She takes his hand in hers and holds it tight against the place of his lingering touch. Tears wet her round eyes, "I'm so sorry that I wasn't here with you the last time."

"I know."

"I'm not leaving this time."

"I know."

Annie lays her head on Mike's bed and falls asleep while he plays with the long silky strands of her hair. When Michael Monopoli is sure that Annie Mahoney-Maxwell can no longer hear his words, he whispers, "I love you, Sweet Annie."

From Netti to Nowhere
Fred has had enough. Without explanation, he gets up, walks out of the farmhouse to his F-150, grunts to Veronica's muscle, "Move the damn Discovery," and backs out of the driveway. Normally, he would head down Farm Road Low

toward the bungalow he shares with Kitt. Tonight he heads to I-95N. He puts his tunes on – the pedal to the metal – and miles and miles of distance between him and the shit he thought he left behind. He quickly racks up physical distance, but mental distance, not so much.

"You or my job. That's it? You're giving me no other options?"

"No."

"Seriously, that's it? This is where we are, Serp?"

"This is where I am, Roni. I don't want to do this. I can't do this."

"What's changed?"

"I've changed, the problem is that you haven't." **Fred closed the physical space between them, took her hands in his,** "Roni, the field work, you're addicted to it. You don't have to be onsite for the raids, but you can't not be there—you can't stay away from the pits of Hell. The laws of averages say you aren't gonna come home one day. I don't want to be here when the knock comes."

"Serp, I could say the same about you and your job."

"You could, but we both know it's a false equivalency."

"So, you'd rather be alone?"

"No, Roni, I don't want to be alone. I don't want to be without you, but…"

"But we can only be together if I give it all up, if I choose you."

"Yes."

Roni pulled her hands away, ran one through her cropped hair. Her light green eyes showed her anguish, her words cut through it, "I want you, Serp, but I…"

"—choose the job," he finished her sentence.

"Yes."

Fred Serpico left Veronica Shields that night. The instant she heard the door close behind him, she begged the universe, "Please have him ask again. I'll choose him. Please."

He didn't ask again—he never saw her again. He filed for divorce, took custody of the East Coast and nothing else, and agreed to a "no show" court proceeding. When he got the call from his lawyer, the newly single Fred Serpico hopped into his new F-150, and headed east. He put a Seger CD in—shuffled through the tunes—played the ones that touched a chord—then the ones that set him free.

A few hours after Fred left the farmhouse, he's back in Mayflower, and heading toward Laurel Falls. That's when the shit that's been banging in his head for two damned years hits the fan. "I wanted Roni to choose her job."

Bullet Bungalow

103

The bedroom light is on when Fred arrives home. It's on because Maura woke Kitt to tell her about the Halle Berry lookalike.

"I can explain," he says as he walks into the room.

"Good. Start by explaining that your ex-wife is a Halle Berry clone." Kitt is suddenly having a **big** problem with doppelgangers.

"Are you upset because Roni is black?"

"Don't be ridiculous. I'm upset that your ex-wife looks like H.a.l.l.e. B.e.r.r.y."

"I probably should have mentioned that, but…"

She yawns in his face.

"Kittridge…"

She yawns in his face.

The relieved man and the exhausted woman agree to table their discussion until the next morning because she's yawned four times since Mr. Halle Berry walked into the bedroom. Kitt stomps to the California king, grabs an elastic, and twists her hair into a messy bun— Just. So. She. Can. Hear. His. Moan. She plops onto the bed, moves to her side, pulls the covers high, and mutters a few choice words before drifting off. The last two are caught in a yawn, "Halilue Berryah."

Completely undone.

Kitt woke early. Very early. She spent a good amount of time pacing the room and is now standing at the bedroom window looking out at the Atlantic. It is appropriately rage churning.

Fred slips from bed and moves as close as humanly possible behind her. He reaches around and places his hand onto her belly and brushes her neck with kisses. "I'm where I want to be."

"I know."

"Why are you upset?"

"Because I'm pregnant. Because I'm hormonal. Because there's so much about you I don't know."

Fred takes Kitt's hand, "Let's sit. You can ask me anything."

"Did you love, Veronica?" The words have tumbled before she's thought them through. "That was a stupid question. Of course, you loved her. You were married to her for a long time. Tell me why you aren't together anymore."

"I loved her, admired her, and I wanted to change her."

"Change her? That doesn't sound like you, Fred. You seem so accepting of people."

"There came a time when I couldn't accept her job anymore. It was exciting in the beginning; she loved it and was very good at it. But after years of undercover assignments that took her to the pits of Hell, it wasn't exciting anymore. I pointed out the dangers associated with her job – she did the same with mine. I recognized the hypocrisy of the situation, but at the end of the day, I saw her job as being way more perilous than mine. When I got to the breaking point, I gave Roni an ultimatum: me or the job. She said she wanted me, but she chose the job."

Kitt crawls onto Fred's lap. He takes her hand and threads their fingers together.

"Do you still love her?"

"Roni was my friend, my wife, my family. I will always love her on some level, but I am not in love with her. The truth is, I fell out of love with Roni a long time before I gave her that ultimatum. There's another truth, Kittridge. I love you, and I am in love with you. I told you that I am all in, and I am. There is no going back for me. I moved on from Roni long before I met you. And from the moment I met you, I hoped I'd be moving forward with you."

Kitt knows she should leave it there, but she doesn't, "And, when you saw her last night, how did you feel?"

"My heart skipped a beat."

Kitt's heart skips several beats. Big drops of water roll down her cheeks. Fred wipes them away with his thumbs then takes her face in his hands. She closes her eyes and lets the tears flow. She couldn't stop them if she tried, so she doesn't try.

"Kittridge, listen to me, look at me. My heart skipped a beat because Roni is a stunningly beautiful woman, and I am a red-blooded man. Veronica Shields affects men— she affected each of the men in that room last night. My heart skipped when I saw her, but my heart belongs to the stunningly beautiful woman who shared my bed last night. You, Kittridge Mahoney, have completely undone me."

She gets off Fred's lap, crawls back into bed, and reaches out to him. They leave one another completely undone.

Farm Road

Turner Blakely's cell phone plays the theme from *Taxi Driver* until his voicemail is full and his battery is dead. The young cabbie didn't report back in with dispatch after his dinner break, nor did he answer his friends' cell phone calls or texts. Turner Blakely won't answer any more calls or return any more texts. He will leave something for the police, though.

Netti

Joy's taskforce meets precisely at 10 AM. John put his coffee percolator to work making a dozen cups to go with the dozen donuts Steve brought from Perks. When the taskforce is sufficiently hyped up on sugar and caffeine, they assemble around the table. Fred starts, "I think we should take Roni through Joy's list, and get her up to speed." The detective hands his ex-wife the paper with Joy's death words on it. He waits while she reads it.

"I see why you've been looking at this as a series of clues. This isn't emotional. I would imagine a woman leaving a child, particularly one she never knew; and leaving the man she loved forever, would say things specific to them. Tell me what you've come up with."

"First up, (John do list). We're thinking this is a directive to look at an alphabetical list of yearly reunions John and Joy took every August. The list…"

Roni interrupts, "I know about the list, Fred, please continue."

"Right. You knew Joy Ann Watts." He lets the sentence hang, then moves on, "Joy's directive was for John to **do** the list, not **repeat** the list. We figure she was referring to places that came after Madrid. Seattle jumped out as sort of an equation: Seattle = Roni = DEA = Hector. The equation continued after Joy's death: Hector = Montoya = Hitman = Mayflower."

Roni nods.

"Next up, (pink and white). Tess Maxwell has godawful pink and white chevron wallpaper in her bedroom. Joy spent her last night alive in that room. There is every reason to think that the wallpaper was seared into her memory, but we think we've connected it to another clue. I'll get to that later. Next up, (go deep). Joy lived deep in cyberland. We figured there was a reason she wanted us to go there. When John went deep..."

"I learned that the FBI is still working the Hector case, even though there is no Hector. Then I learned that drug syndicates have waged war on the DEA. Joy couldn't have known any of that at the time of her death, but her directive for us to (go deep) led to the information. There could be more in cyberland, so another dive is in my future."

Fred jumps back in. "Next up, (Kitt thank you save Tess). Kittridge said that Joy uttered all of this as a single thought or sentence. We've gone back and forth on what Joy meant. The general consensus right now is that she was putting out a call to Kitt to help (save Tess). Admittedly, this part needs work before we can make complete sense of it. Next up, (Fred message). On the morning of the shooting, when I found out that Annie was kidnapped, and two MFPD officers were injured, I called everyone to the kitchen. Joy was the last one getting there because she came from Tess' upstairs bedroom. When she got near, she took hold of my arm to stop me from leaving. She said, 'Fred, I need to tell...' She never had the chance to finish that sentence. We've been pulling at that thread, and this is where we are right now. When John went deep, he found out that Joy crashed her system **before** she came downstairs that morning. We think something happened when she was upstairs, and that she might have wanted to tell me about it, OR she left me a message in Tess' (pink and white) room. That's where we left off last night. We were going to get back to it after dinner, but…"

"I showed up," Roni finishes Fred's sentence.

"Yeah. Let's move on."

All those assembled get **that** message.

Fred moves on. "Next up, is the word (sorry). This sounds like a ubiquitous statement made by dying people," he throws a dig to his partner for using that word during a previous case.

Steve chucks Fred the finger, "How's this for ubiquitous?"

John and Roni don't get the meaning behind the back and forth.

Fred laughs big. "Next up, (save list Annie system crashed). We agree that the word list might have been an intake of air. If so, we end up with (save Annie system crashed), and lots of possibilities to examine. Did Joy crash her system to (save Annie)? Was she telling us that she crashed her system to (save Tess) and (save Annie)? Did she crash her system because she was leaving FICA and was going to meet Tess? We're still circling the drain on this one."

John addresses Roni, "There are a lot of reasons why Joy might have crashed her system, but we all agree on this: if Joy were compromised, she would have crashed her system, no question. You knew her for a long time, Roni, you must have thoughts on this."

The Special Agent gets up from the table, goes the length of cabinets, and backs into a corner joist.

Fred kicks Steve under the table, "Backing herself into a corner, bet there's a meaning there?"

Steve shoots a look, and a kick of his own.

Roni pulls a breath and gives a slight nod, "My secret friendship with Joy spanned more than a dozen years. We kept in touch when we first left Quantico. That wasn't an issue, but when Joy went Dead On Assignment, she was supposed to end all of her relationships, except for the one she had with John Maxwell. We knew we were breaking DEA and FICA protocol by maintaining a friendship, but she did it because she found her life very isolating. I suppose I did it for the same reason. Female agents, even those who aren't Dead On Assignment, have difficulties with friendships because there are so many things that can't be shared or discussed. Simply put, barriers are impediments to friendship. Given that the stakes were high for us, Joy and I set rules for our illicit liaison: we would never tell anyone about our friendship, we would discuss personal things only, and the cornerstone would be complete honesty.

"I'm telling you because I want you to know that I **knew** Joy. What I say shouldn't be taken with a grain of salt, it should be received as fact. Joy was deeply conflicted about staying out of Tess' life. It had gotten to the point where she was reevaluating her role at FICA. She said that she'd started feeling as though something at the Agency was off, that she was picking up on some sort of current. She always knew that she worked in the shadow of the Boy Genius and was quick to laugh about it, but she said that something at the Agency had changed, and it was affecting her standing, somehow."

Fred and Steve try really hard not to look at John. They fail.

Roni finishes her thought. "Joy crossed the line between personal and professional when Gaffney put a team of agents in to help deal with Hector. She said it really unnerved her that people were looking for DOA, even if they were Agency people. It was the only time that I sensed a vibe of vulnerability coming from the almighty DOA. If Joy had an itch that something was off at FICA, then we should start there. And since Joy lived in cyberland, I think we should look there."

"Before we do anything, let's break," Fred says, as he heads to the living room window.

Amongst other things.

Maura bursts into Kitt's kitchen with a shovel and a tarp, "Where's the body?"

"What body," she asks laughing.

"Fred's body," Maura scans the kitchen. "You didn't kill him?"

"Why would I kill Fred? He can't help it if Veronica is pretty."

"Gorgeous," Kitt's Best Fucking Friend corrects.

"Is that what Steve told you?" asking, but not really wanting to know.

Maura nods, "Amongst other things."

Kitt Mahoney quickly ponders whether she wants to hear what Steve had to say on the subject of Fred's ex-wife. **Of course she wants to hear**. "Spill. And don't leave out a single thing," she stupidly encourages.

"According to Steve, Veronica, or Roni as Fred calls her, is Halle Berry gorgeous with long, long, supermodel legs. He drooled—I mean he said—that she's at least 5'11" tall, totally cut from hours in the gym, has buzz cut black hair, light green eyes, caramel-colored skin, and a sexuality that is off the charts." Maura's lips stop flapping long enough for her eyes to open and notice Kitt's face—the one that **is not** Halle Berry gorgeous. Maura can't pull back her words, so she adds insult to injury by trying some new ones on for size. "Oh, Kitt, don't worry. You're very pretty, you know—Evangeline Lilly pretty. But better. And you're smart and accomplished. You're a wonderful mom. And ooooo, ooooo, you're pregnant with Fred's baby."

"Jesus, Maura, why don't you just bludgeon me with your shovel and tarp my body?"

Kitt is alone when she visits Annie at Mayflower-Falls Regional. Callie and Tess are at a basketball thing at the high school, and their Auntie Maura, the woman with whom Kitt is no longer speaking, is getting them from there and hanging out with them for a while. That way Kitt can hang out with Annie, and visit with Mike. She pushes into her daughter's hospital room, hands off the computer she asked for, and tosses a change of clothes onto her lap with a brusque, "Here."

Annie grunts, "Thanks. I think."

"Any news on when you can leave the hospital?" Kitt asks, not bothering to feign any interest in her daughter's answer—the daughter who is in a hospital—recovering from a concussion.

"Mom!"

"What!?"

"I'm…"

Kitt drifts into the conversation she's been having with herself, *I wonder what the 6' tall black goddess is doing. Working with, OR on, my 6'2" man? Is she really in Mayflower because of a case, OR—*

"…Mom!"

"Sorry. Did you say something?"

"I thanked you for the clothes and the computer, and I said that I'm getting discharged late this afternoon, but since Mike isn't going to be discharged until tomorrow, I'm going to camp out in his room tonight, and that the computer will help if I can't sleep. You didn't hear any of that?" The daughter stares at the mother, tilts her head to one side, and does a bit of scrutinizing. "Mom, are you alright? Is the baby alright?"

Kitt smiles at Annie's reference to the baby. "We're fine, Annie. Thank you for asking."

"Then, what's wrong."

Kitt makes a quick pact with herself that she is not going to admit to her 21-year-old daughter that she is jealous of a woman she hasn't seen or met. She quickly breaks the pact. "I think I'm jealous of Fred's ex-wife," she sheepishly confesses.

Annie scoffs, "I'd be jealous, too. It's not every day a 6' tall Halle Berry comes to Mayflower."

Kitt groans. Kitt leaves. Kitt stops by to see Mike, who is sitting in a chair watching a rebroadcast of a Patriots game on a 6" by 6" television. He starts to get up when she walks in.

"Please don't get up. You get points for thinking about it though."

He smiles. He has a nice smile.

"How are you feeling? You look really good."

"I'm good to go, Ms. Mahoney."

"Call me Kitt. I think you've earned it by saving Annie," she million-watts him. "I would give you a big hug if it wouldn't cause you pain, so I'll hold off for now, but remind me."

Mike smiles again, "Will do, Kitt."

The mother of Annie Mahoney-Maxwell watches a bit of the game with the guy who has captured her daughter's heart. She breaks the easy silence with a fit of the giggles. "I'm sorry, Mike. You do know that you're a doppelganger of Danny Amendola, right?"

"Annie mentioned that once or twice."

Kitt points to the petite television, "Look at Danny, he's your mini-me." She hasn't a clue why this strikes her as being really funny—but this strikes her as being really funny.

Mike gets up after a minute of her giggling, "Would you like me to get Annie for you, Ms. Kitt?"

She laughs herself into a fit of tears, "Nope, nope, I'm good," she says before leaving.

THE CARTEL

Marco Martinez follows a fiery red Cadillac CTS from Mayflower-Falls Regional High School to a white two-story Victorian on Primrose Lane. A beautiful redhead and twin teenage girls goof around as they walk to the house. It is the perfect opportunity for him to grab his mark, but he doesn't know which of the two girls is Tess Maxwell. His life depends on not fucking up, so he calls his boss—he gets voicemail. "Twins? You didn't say she's a twin," Marco drives away muttering. "How am I supposed to know which one to take? And he better not say he wants both of them."

He is still waiting for a return call from Paulo Montoya when the redhead and the twins get back into the Caddie, scoot around Mayflower, stop at Perks and a corner mini mart, and pull onto the driveway at the bungalow. Marco watches the three of them run around to the back of the house. "Fuck it! I'll shoot the Jessica Rabbit lookalike, take the twins, and get the fuck out of Massachusetts. Montoya can figure out the rest." He starts to inch toward the bungalow, stops when a brunette in a white RAV4 pulls onto the driveway followed by an MFPD police cruiser. Marco inches away from the beachfront neighborhood.

They're together.

The L-Ride Cab Company uses GPS to locate Turner Blakely's cab. It's in Mayflower. The company dispatcher contacts MFPD dispatch and asks that a patrol car do a wellness check on their missing cabbie.

Netti
Joy's taskforce sets a plan of action and divides the workload. (John do list) does not need action at this time. (Pink and white) and (Fred message) needs immediate work and will be handled by Fred. (Go deep) and (Annie system crashed) also needs immediate work and will be handled by John. Steve and Roni are going to focus their attention on the dead non-Caucasian, Carlos Montoya. The team wants to know how long he was in Mayflower and what he was up to during that time.

Before they disband for the day, Roni asks for a few minutes. She leans herself into the corner joist, again. "I want to give you a broader understanding of why I'm on the East Coast. When Hector was killed, the cartels no longer had the upper hand over the Feds. The DEA moved swiftly and executed two raids that had been in the works. The raids were very successful; we got the goods, the weapons cache, the money, and a few upper level dealers. Without the aid of Hector, the syndicates and the Feds were back on level playing field. The response from the cartels was swift. Competing drug families formed an association with one specific goal: kill as many DEA agents as possible. The brain behind this unholy alliance is Paulo Montoya. As you know, Montoya is East Coast drugs, but his move toward banding competing organizations suggested that he is interested in branching out. In response to his apparent jockeying to become head of a regional cartel, the powers-that-be at the DEA moved as many agents and resources as they could to the eastern seaboard.

"That's how I ended up in New York. Last week a group of DEA agents were ambushed inside a Greenwich Village restaurant. After the bloodbath, two agents were dead, killed execution style in a bathroom. Several others, including myself, made it out by the skin of our teeth. Apparently, Montoya put a bounty on three Special Agents who were there that night. I was included in that select group. I am the only one who made it out alive. The FBI agents outside are my protective duty."

Roni looks directly at Fred, "Serp, I have been authorized to work the case from your angle. Whatever resources or information you require from the DEA are at your disposal. Are there any questions, gentlemen?"

"Yeah. What restaurant in Greenwich Village?"

Roni starts to laugh at her ex-husband, then hangs her head when the tears sting.

Fred gets up and goes to his ex-wife. He pulls her from the corner joist, and into his arms. "I'm sorry, Roni."

"I'm sorry, Serp."

They are sorry for two very different reasons.

Mayflower-Falls Regional

Annie is discharged from the hospital just before dinner and goes directly to Mike's room, happy to find Cluster and Jane visiting. Both Annie and Mike were put in private rooms after the accident, most likely courtesy of Maura, who seems to run the hospital. Mike's private room is plenty big enough for the little gathering that is taking place, and it's a corner room so there's extra privacy. That will come in handy later when Annie wants to stowaway overnight.

Cluster goes down to the cafeteria and grabs cheeseburgers, fries, and sodas all around. Mike reminds the big bear of a man and his lovely Southern belle that they are on "get the Christmas tree out of my condo" duty on the second of January. That conversation leads to an invitation for Cluster and Jane to join Mike and Annie for New Year's Eve. Since the injured cop and his girl are recliner-bound for the duration, Cluster and Jane score the bedroom. Annie Mahoney-Maxwell smiles wide at the thought of ringing in the New Year with her man.

Farm Road
Officer Grant Speil searches for the missing L-Ride cab. He finds it a quarter mile from John Maxwell's farmhouse, and calls it in. He requests that Serpico and Phelps be notified.

The MFPD detectives leave the farmhouse just as the sun is calling it a day. They meet Officer Speil at the scene of a car off the road with one fatality. Both men have been taking a few days off during the holidays, but they show at the scene of suspicious deaths. From the looks of things, the fatality isn't suspicious, it's a homicide.

Speil updates the detectives, "At approximately 1600 hours, MFPD dispatch received a call from L-Ride cab company out of Boston. Their GPS showed the location of a missing cab in this area. The driver had not been heard from since dinner break the day before, at 1530 hours. I conducted a drive by at the GPS location at approximately 1610 hours. I found tracks in snow-covered foliage along the shoulder of Farm Road. Further investigation revealed a yellow cab off the road and down a slight hilled section of land. I approached the vehicle and observed a deceased male, the victim of an apparent gunshot wound."

Fred and Steve make note that the cab is on John's property, then they notice lights come on at Netti Barn off in the distance.

Netti
John takes Veronica to the barn while Fred and Steve are on the MFPD call. The DEA Special Agent looks around while the FICA Special Agent checks on "some things". Having read FBI and police reports of the shooting of Joy Ann Watts, Veronica knows where in Netti Barn she wants to be. John finds her there several minutes later.

"I haven't been up here since that day."

"I hope you don't mind my coming up."

"You're standing where Hector was when he took the kill shot of Joy, and where I almost lost my daughter, Annie. This is where I was standing when I shot the fucker."

"Annie, she's your daughter with Kitt Mahoney?" She asks, though she already knows.

"Yes."

"May I ask you a question?" Veronica has turned to face John—the upcoming topic of discussion written on her face.

"Not if it's about Kitt," he answers firmly.

"Understood. How about I ask you about Fred, then?"

John pauses long before saying, "To be honest, it's the same as asking me about Kitt. They're together, Roni."

The ex-wife turns back to the darkened window and silently processes.

The prospect of keystroking.

The discharge process of Officer Monopoli begins shortly before 8 AM. His surgeon doesn't bat-an-eye when Annie emerges from the shower in Mike's room. The doc smiles—signs the discharge papers—and throws a cautionary word or two, "Take it easy for a few days, Michael."

"I'll take it any way I can get it, doc."

"Then I'll expect to see you again, Michael."

John is waiting at the hospital for Annie and Mike. He was surprised when his daughter called him for a lift to Mike's condo. Pleasantly surprised. After getting them settled in the SUV, he listens as Annie motor-mouths a recap of the "ride from hell" as she refers to the event that sent her back to the ER. When there's a lull in conversation John wades in, "So, Annie, I heard that you haven't gone online since Hector."

"Nope. But I asked Mom to bring my computer to the hospital. I'm ready to play around. I didn't have time last night, but maybe later today. I can't wait. I think my fingers are actually itching at the prospect of keystroking." Annie leans forward in her seat and addresses Mike, "You probably heard from Cluster or

Jane," she pauses and addresses her father, "and you probably heard from Mom or Fred, that I took a leave of absence from Littleton this semester. I needed to get my head on straight, figure out what I want, and what's important," Annie smiles big at Mike. "I figured it all out."

Mike smiles big at Annie.

John smiles big, inside.

Boston

The ex-wife of Fred Serpico wakes to an empty bed, in a strange hotel, in a strange city, with a drug lord's bounty on her head. None of that matters. The thing that tortured Veronica Shields, the thing that kept her up most of the night, is the finality behind the words she doubts she will ever forget.

"They're together, Roni."

Bullet Bungalow

Fred is woken to the muffled sounds of morning sickness coming from the en suite. He hustles from bed, and gives a gentle knock on the locked door, "Kittridge."

"Leave."

"Can I help?"

"Yes. You can leave," She growls. She retches. She gretches.

He reluctantly does as he's told, but only because there was a threat of bodily harm, involving a knee to a groin. "It's gonna be a l.o.n.g. nine months," he laughs on his way out of the bedroom. He arrives at the kitchen just in time to hear Steve's knock on the back door. The visiting detective starts talking the instant the door swings open.

"You make coffee, I'll do a quick update on the trip Grant and I took to Turner Blakey's place. We talked to his mother and sister, they couldn't have been kinder, or more proud of Turner. My gut says that this kid was as clean as they come…"

As requested by Detective Phelps, Officer Speil arrives at the bungalow at 0800 hours, the case file on the Farm Road shooting in hand.

"Give us what you've got, Speil," Steve says.

"Before you start, let's move this into the living room," Fred tilts his head in the direction of the master bedroom, "Ms. Mahoney isn't feeling right this morning."

The men settle. The officer begins. "Turner Blakely was a 21-year-old commuter student at Boston University. He lived at home in Jamaica Plains with his mother and younger sister. He attended BU on a generous academic and athletic scholarship. He helped defray uncovered college expenses, and provide financially for his family, by driving for L-Ride, a cab company that operates exclusively out of Logan International Airport. According to Turner's fare log, his last run was a pick up at the airport at 1510 hours, with a drop off at State Street Bank. L-Ride dispatch reported that Turner requested an early dinner break, which put him off the clock beginning at 1530 hours. The cabbie never clocked back in, did not answer calls from dispatch, nor from any family members or friends for a 24-hour period, at which time L-Ride GPS tracked the cab to Mayflower and notified MFPD.

"A preliminary Medical Examiner's report puts time of death at approximately 1730 hours yesterday, approximately two hours after he clocked out. Turner Blakely died from a single, close range gunshot wound with no other visible signs of injury. Personal possessions found in the cab are the victim's wallet with a Massachusetts driver's license, an ATM card, $43 cash, a cell phone, and a backpack containing textbooks, several pens, and notebooks. Cab company items found are an unopened L-Ride cashbox, his fare log on the passenger seat, and his identification placard hanging from the rearview mirror."

Fred addresses the young officer. "What's next, Speil?"

"Come again, Detective?"

"Officer Speil, I would like you to run the case. What is your next step?"

"I think we can rule out robbery because the victim's wallet and money, and the company cashbox were in the cab. That's the only thing that's conclusive," Speil says.

Steve joins the conversation, "What if the perp didn't want the cash? What if there was something else in the car, and that was what the perp wanted. That might constitute a robbery, right?"

"There's nothing to indicate there was anything taken from the car, Detective Phelps."

"Nothing to say otherwise. The point I'm making, Speil, is that it's too early to rule out anything."

The detectives have Officer Speil take a seat in the living room, then begin teaching.

Cutters

John walks Mike and Annie to the condo on the guise of helping the walking wounded, but the law enforcement professional, who is also a protective father, wants to see where his daughter is staying and whether the place is secure. "Officer Monopoli, this is basic security. You'll need to get **protection** if Annie's going to spend time here." John drills the young man with his eyes.

Mike gets the point—both of the intended points. "Protection, yes sir. Consider it done, sir."

Annie rolls her eyes at her father, sends him a full-on grin, a raised hand to her heart, and a singsong, "Isn't he wonderful?"

John rolls his eyes at his daughter.

She hip-chucks him, "I am one of three John Maxwell children conceived without **protection**. I will handle the birth control, thank you very much!"

Mike groans.

John growls.

Annie smirks.

Bullet Bungalow

Kitt has been sitting in the kitchen nibbling square salt crackers and listening to her man teach a potential detective for nearly an hour.

"Officer Speil, investigations are about finding answers to questions. Tell me what questions you have."

"Yes, sir. Why did Turner take an early dinner break? Why did he drive an hour away when he only had an hour break? Is he regularly late returning from dinner?"

Fred stops Speil, "Officer, those are all valid questions. I suggest you find answers to them. See who's available, and the two of you head to L-Ride for the answers. And find out why L-Ride waited 24-hours before notifying MFPD."

Office Speil hightails it past Kitt, sight unseen, as does Detective Phelps. Fred hasn't seen her either and is opening the bedroom door when she speaks from over his shoulder. "Are you looking for me Detective Serpico?"

Fred turns, his smile cutting his dimples deep, "Why, yes I am."

"Good, because I've been waiting to give you something."

"Is that so?"

The seductress gets up from the table, takes a few steps across the kitchen, all the while untying her robe. She is stark naked, her pregnancy breasts fuller than usual, her belly starting to show their creation. Fred's smile grows with each step she takes, each moves she makes. When he can stand it no longer, he closes the space between them, sweeps her into his arms, and heads to their bedroom, kicking the door shut behind him.

THE CARTEL

Marco and the two goons spent part of the night driving around Mayflower, and part of the night in a cheap motel on the outskirts of town. They were back on Farm Road in time to see a guy leaving the yellow farmhouse. Driver goon followed the black BMW to Mayflower-Falls Regional, and after waiting twenty minutes they watched farmhouse guy load two injured people into the SUV. Driver goon followed the threesome to a building on Slater, drove past the place, spun around, and backtracked. They've been sitting just beyond the parking lot since, waiting for farmhouse guy to leave Cutters Cove.

Whatever-your-middle-name-is.

Steve and Veronica are waiting at the farmhouse when John arrives.

"Sorry, I'm late. I had a tail. A black Escalade was waiting for me outside Mike Monopoli's condo building. It was at the hospital when I picked up Annie and Mike, but if it tailed me from there, I didn't catch it. The tail knew I made him at the condos, and pulled back when I approached the intersection of Slater and Crenshaw."

Steve pulls his cell from his pocket, "I'll have a patrol car do a drive by Mike's, maybe the tail has something to do with them?"

John opens the farmhouse, "Hey, Steve, where's Fred?"

"We were just at the bungalow working the cabbie homicide. When I left, he was right behind me. He must have gotten sidetracked."

Everyone in the room has their suspicions as to what sidetracked Fred. Their suspicions are confirmed when Mr. Happy Pants breezes in an hour late. "Okay," he begins with a clap. "Let's talk about the homicide within a stone's throw from this farmhouse. Steve, you're up."

"Already covered most of it, Fred. I'm just getting to the ME's report."

"Carry on, partner."

"A preliminary report puts the time of death at approximately 1730 hours. Turner Blakely died from a single, close range gunshot wound with no other visible signs of injury. Officer Speil is on his way to L-Ride to ask a few questions..."

Roni interrupts Steve, "You might want to have him check Turner's fare log heading out of Logan the day I arrived. My bodyguard thought we might have picked up a tail, but dismissed it because it was a cab."

Fred jumps in, "The threads I want us to pull right now are: why was a Boston cabbie murdered a quarter mile from a farmhouse in Mayflower, Massachusetts—where a DEA agent from Seattle, Washington—currently working out of New York City—who barely escaped a syndicate-ordered execution—was visiting at the time of the cabbie's murder?"

Cutters

Annie calls her mother for the name of the security company that put in the systems at Bullet Bungalow. Mike, who's standing at Annie's back pulls her tight against him when she disconnects.

"Is your mom sick?" A nibble to her neck. A touch here.

"No, why do you ask?" Giggle. Giggle.

"Because you asked her how she is feeling," A nibble to her neck. A touch there.

Annie spins from Mike's embrace, her face, neck, and arms are fully flushed.

Mike takes one look at Annie and knows that her flush **is not** from a touch here or there. "Holy shit, the detective and your mom are preggers!"

Annie squares off and wags her finger in his face, "Michael whatever-your-middle-name-is Monopoli, you are not to tell a single soul. Do you understand me?"

Mike nods and laughs, "Hey, Annie, you let the Kitt-en out of the bag."

Annie groans.

Hanlon from Breens Security arrives at 2 PM to install a security system. He is chuckling before he even steps foot into 2A, "Cutters doesn't usually allow individual units to get their own systems, but they gave immediate approval for you, Officer Monopoli. They said I'd better slap this sucker in, before there's another gunfight at Cutters Coral," he laughs.

Annie and Mike join in on the laugh, then step into the hall for a little less human contact. They find that that is going to be impossible. Every other second floor condo resident is already in the hall buzzing about Breens Security. Amongst the assembled loiterers is a somewhat nosey old lady from 2B, a somewhat gruff redneck dude and his tall, tanned, toned wife from 2C, and newlyweds from 2D—who

Mike hasn't met—but who he's heard—frequently. Missing from the wacky weirdos is the old lady's spinster daughter.

"Michael dear," old lady Bodreau begins, "are you expecting another gunfight? Is that why you're putting in that security thing?"

Mike chuckles, "No, Mrs. Bodreau. My girl's dad wants me to keep her extra safe. I'm just following orders."

"Good. Always listen to your girl's father. Is this your girl? She sure is a pretty, little thing. What's your name, honey?"

"It's Annie, Mrs. Bodreau."

"Michael bring her around for dinner. I'll make your favorite meatloaf and baked potatoes. And bring around that friend of yours for my daughter."

Sneade from 2C chimes in, "Hey, Mike, my wife was a pretty little thing once." The redneck laughs big.

His wife playfully smacks him across his shoulder, "Yeah, well your pretty, little thing ain't worth discussing."

The newlyweds, Mr. and Mrs. Buck from 2D don't join the conversation. The wife is eyeing her man like he's a tree she wants to climb, and the mighty sequoia looks as though he can't wait for the ascent.

When Annie and Mike close their condo door behind them an hour later, Annie bursts into a fit of laughter, "Well, **that** was interesting!"

"I bet I can make it more interesting," Mike challenges.

"Impossible, but I accept your challenge."

"What's the wager?"

"You name it."

"Fantasy sex act. Once my brace is off."

"Deal! Now make what happened in the hall more interesting."

Mike grins from ear to ear, the corners of his eyes become a crinkled mess of smile lines. "Everyone in that hall, except for us, is related."

"Oh. My. God."

Mike growls and moves in on his girl, "I think those are gonna be the words I use after you make good on your bet."

Annie starts paying up front, "To the behemoth, Mr. Monopoli."

Netti

Detective Phelps has Officer Speil come to the farmhouse to update the taskforce on the Turner Blakely homicide. As soon as the young officer walks in, he knows he's amongst law enforcement royalty: two highly decorated detectives, two Special Agents, one with the FBI, and the other with the DEA. He also knows he'd better deliver.

"Tell us what you've got, Officer."

"I spoke with the owners of L-Ride, Donna and Clark Davenport. Mrs. Davenport was the dispatcher on duty the night Turner Blakely requested an early dinner break. She said she granted his request because he hadn't asked for a minute of time off since he began driving for them eighteen months ago. Mrs. Davenport has no idea why he wanted to break early, and based on his employment record, she expected him back driving within an hour's time. When he didn't clock back in, she put him off the clock thinking he had some sort of personal emergency. She never thought he'd be dead in some field in Mayflower.

"Clark Davenport said Turner was studying journalism, and criminology and said he kept a notebook full of observations that he made on his fares. He said it was Turner's way of getting ready for investigative reporting. Davenport suggested that we check Turner's notebooks, that we might find something that'll help our investigation."

The taskforce disbands for the afternoon. Steve and Speil head to MFPD to read the notebooks of a murdered BU student. Fred heads to Bullet Bungalow to look for a message from a murdered FICA Special Agent. Veronica heads to her hotel to take a nap. John heads to Netti Barn to take a dive.

THE CARTEL

"What?"

"Boss, the chica is a twin. I have no clue which one to take."

"Take them both."

"I'm gonna need more people, and better than the goons I'm with now. The girls are always with someone, and there's a patrol car driving around their neighborhood." Marco steps over a line, "Boss, we don't need the chica let alone two of them."

"The chica is leverage," his snarls.

"You won't need leverage. I'll make sure the computer puta does what you want. I might even have some fun keeping her in line."

"Forget the pussy, concentrate on the job."

"The puta **is** the job, and she's accessible. I could snatch her, and we'd have what you need, a new Hector."

"Shut up, Marco." The crime lord takes a minute, then barks, "I'll call you back." Montoya puts his Luger and his cell on his desk. Lifts a spoon. Takes a snort. Lifts a spoon. Takes a snort. He moves about his office, getting angrier by the second, "I want **both** daughters of Joy Ann Watts and John Maxwell. I told Hector that I'd make them pay—every fucking day of their miserable fucking lives if they killed my cyber-drug-savior." The implacable enemy of Special Agent Maxwell takes another hit, then slams his hand onto the desktop, sending the rest of his cut coke skyward in a plume of white. "I need to send a message to the other syndicates—Paulo Montoya is in charge. That won't happen if I don't have a replacement for Hector."

He grabs his Luger, walks out onto a patio, and fires three shots into the trunk of a palm tree. He fires two more shots obliterating two fronds that dislodged from the crown and started floating downward. His thinking becomes rapid, his words, heated. "The DEA bitch went to Mayflower to make sure my stupido nephew is dead. That makes sense, but that's not why she's still there. Maybe Special Agent Maxwell is fucking Special Agent Shields. That makes sense, but that doesn't explain the two detectives that have been hanging around the farmhouse." He pauses. He thinks. He concludes. "The four of them are working on something, and it's not just the death of Carlos."

The drug lord takes one more shot at the palm, walks into his office, paces and reconciles a few things. "Fucking Marco. He thinks he is so smart. The fucker hasn't once asked why I want **these** two girls. Why I want **this** computer puta. Not once has he asked why the DEA bitch is hanging out at a farm in Mayflower. Not once has he asked who owns the farmhouse. The stupido hasn't made the connection between

John Maxwell, Joy Ann Watts, and the computer puta. He must be fucked up on blow. I better send some backup for the job, and when I have my new Hector, I'm gonna kill that mutha-fucking Marco."

Montoya puts down his Luger, and picks up his cell. "Get the cyber puta. You've got 48-hours. And Marco, don't come back to Miami if you screw up—and don't bother trying to hide."

This godforsaken place.

Bullet Bungalow is empty when Fred gets home. He goes directly to Tess' room and stands at the doorway. He runs his hand along his chin scruff, eyes the window across the room, and ponders an easy out, "I could jump," he laughs. He does a study of the room, "Standard fare for a teenager: bed, end table, bureau, desk with straight-back chair, coatrack, and closet." *Vampire Diaries* posters and a peg board are the only wall coverings. "I'd cover every damn inch of this crap." He takes a slower look at the furnishings, searching for anomalies, anything that seems out of place; added on, taken off. "Joy spent approximately eight hours in this room. She probably spent half of that time sleeping, which means some of that time was spent learning about Tess. And if we are right, she spent some of her time crashing her FICA system." He stands at Tess' window processing for a few, then turns back, "Joy crashed her system. Her computer system. Where is Joy's computer?"

Fred is on his hands and knees when Tess runs into her room. "Great, you're home, I followed a mouse up here. I think it's under your bed. Help me get it."

"A mouse! Fred, not a mouse! I'm not helping. And I'm not sleeping in here until you find it! But don't kill it, okay?" Tess bolts from the room.

"Like a mouse would come into this godforsaken place."

Cutters

Annie is nestled into the behemoth when she has the urge to get online. She's just put her computer onto her lap, and is ready to get at it when Mike comes into the living room.

"What's up, Annie?"

"I was just about to do a little keystroking."

The randy young man bends toward his girl and tilts her head back, "Please tell me that's sexual code for something."

Annie puts her computer onto the floor, helps Mike onto the behemoth, and helps herself to Mike.

Boston

John pulls his BMW past the valet service at the Marriott Long Wharf Hotel. He gets out, key fobs the lock, and takes a few minutes looking out at Boston Harbor. "She said dinner. Don't expect more than that from her," he cautions himself. "She was Joy's friend. She was Fred's wife. It's just dinner." By the time he steps off the elevator on her floor, his trademark smirk is on his face, "Who am I kidding—I'm dinner."

Roni was at the window looking at John Maxwell who was looking out at Boston Harbor. She was replaying their earlier conversation through her head.

"Montoya has a bounty out on me, so I'm stuck in my suite. Feel like driving into Boston for dinner?"

She moved away from the window when he headed inside the hotel. She headed to the en suite, did a once over, dabbed a bit of perfume, sloshed some mouthwash, and smiled wide. "Sharing room service with another agent isn't out of the ordinary—having an agent as part of the dinner selection is..."

John turns off his cell, then knocks on Roni's door.

Roni turns off her cell, and answers John's knock.

Chevron Hell

Fred is just about to call it quits when he hits paydirt. A clumsy move getting off the floor of Tess' closet sends him into her coatrack. Jackets, sweatshirts, and duffle bags tumble to a heap on the floor. As Fred starts putting things back on the rack, he notices something written on a white peak on the wall behind it. The words are tiny. Fred gets close and reads: **Callie's room behind bureau**. (Pink and white) is solved! Fred tosses everything back onto the rack, runs across to Callie's room, moves the bureau away from the wall, and finds Joy's computer.

Fred calls John's cell. The call goes directly to voice mail.

The beginning of something big.

Fred is up very early and standing sentry outside the bathroom door. Kitt is behind the closed and locked door. This morning's retch fest is worse than the one the day before, but surprisingly, the heaving woman is less hostile about it. That makes Fred feel worse. "Kittridge, please let me in."

"Fred, I'm alright. Just go back to bed."

"I'm not hitting those sheets until you do."

After a particularly bad series of retching and heaving, Kitt makes a tiny plea, "Please get me some square crackers and a brown soda."

Fred sprints to the kitchen and is back outside the bathroom door in record time. "I've got your crackers and soda, and maybe this will help too, it's snowing. The snowflakes are the big, fat ones you like, Kittridge."

Her man's chipper weather report is met with a protracted series of retching and a warning. "Don't say the words big or fat ever again."

Cutters
Annie is up early, standing in front of the bank of windows, watching big, fat snowflakes fall over the Atlantic Ocean.

"What's so interesting?" Mike asks from across the room.

"It's snowing. It's really beautiful."

Annie hears the lowering of the behemoth, then Mike's footfalls coming near. He brings a blanket with him and wraps it around his girl, embracing her from behind. Many minutes pass without comment.

Boston

John is up early, standing in front of a patio window watching big, fat snowflakes fall over Boston Harbor.

"What's so interesting?" Roni asks from the comfort of a toasty warm bed.

John turns toward the stunning woman he ravaged all night long, "It's snowing. We'd better get back to Mayflower. This looks like the beginning of something big."

THE CARTEL

The goons arrived back in Mayflower shortly before dawn. They brought with them a duffle bag full of weapons and ammunition, and a message from Paulo Montoya, "More goons are on their way."

Marco should have gone back to bed, after all, it's going to be a long day and night, but the hitman is not back in bed. He is standing at a little window, in a little room, in a little Sand 'n Surf motel, on the outskirts of the little seaside community of Mayflower, watching the damn snow fall outside. "Fucking snow!"

The Residents of Mayflower-Laurel Falls

After Fred tucks Kitt back into bed,
he turns on his cell.
After Mike heads to the shower,
Annie boots up her computer.
After John takes another roll with Roni,
he checks his voicemail.

The email is dated October 8.

Fred's cell rings—way before it is acceptable to do so. "It's early, Steve," Fred states the obvious.

Kitt moans and nudges him out of bed. He growls and leaves.

"Have you looked outside?" Steve asks.

"Is this some sort of new MFPD protocol: snowflake alerts?" Fred jokes.

"Not the snow Fred, the detail."

Fred sprints from the bedroom, through the kitchen, through the living room to a window that faces the front and side of the bungalow. He finds a patrol car on the driveway. "What's going on, Steve?"

"John had a tail yesterday, a black Escalade – Turner Blakely wrote in his notebook that he followed a black Escalade from Boston to Mayflower – Speil said he saw a black Escalade on Tarrington near the bungalow. I sent the patrol car to the bungalow a few hours ago. The Escalade is a problem, Fred. Let's get a plan together to save Tess, save Annie, and save the whole fucking lot of you."

"The detail just left."

"Yeah. There's a fucking snowstorm barreling our way. Get your shit together, and call me with a plan, and keep your damn cell on!"

Cutters

Mike comes running from the bedroom when he hears Annie's scream. He finds her crouched deep into the behemoth with her computer on her lap. She is trembling and close to hysteria.

"Annie! What's wrong!?"

She points a shaking finger at her computer screen. Mike reads an email from someone named DOA—sent to Annie—addressed to Fred—from October 8.

> **Fred: Message from Hector. If he gets killed, cartel gets me or Annie as his replacement. Montoya will take Tess for leverage. Save Tess. Save Annie. Unmasked. Crashing system. DOA.**

Mike calls Fred before it is acceptable to do so. "Detective, it's Mike."

"What's up?"

"Annie is in bad shape, Detective. She checked her emails this morning. There's one from DOA. Annie said you'd know what that means. The email is dated October 8. I'm gonna read it to you…Fred: Message from Hector. If he gets killed, cartel gets me or Annie as his replacement. Montoya will take Tess for leverage. Save Tess. Save Annie. Unmasked. Crashing system. DOA."

The penny drops—thousands of pennies drop. (Fred message) is solved! "Monopoli.

Take a picture of the email. Send it to me, Detective Phelps, and John Maxwell in a text. Arm yourself. Get Annie moving. Pack a duffle for each of you. We're putting a plan together to get you and Annie out of the condo. Keep your damn cell on!"

Boston
John listens to the voicemail Fred left the night before. He has no sooner finished when he receives a picture text from Mike Monopoli. It's the email from DOA. His heart bangs hard against his chest. "Roni! Let's move!" Within minutes, he calls Fred from the SUV. "I got DOA's message. What's the plan?"

"I want everyone in one place during the storm. They're forecasting a couple of feet, and it's already starting to pile up. FYI, the Escalade that tailed you has also been seen on Tarrington near the bungalow, and the dead cabbie tailed it from Boston to Mayflower after he picked up one of the Escalade passengers from Logan. You'd better get ready. You're gonna have a houseful of guests within the hour."

"Fred, tell Annie to let everyone in. She knows the security system."

"You're not at the farmhouse?"

"No. I'm on my way there, now."

There is a pause from Fred. "You on the way in from Boston?"

"Yes."

"Is Roni with you?"

"Yes."

Fred ends the call and immediately makes another. He updates Steve on everything—except for the John banging Roni part. By the end of their conversation Steve agrees with Fred's plan: Get everyone to Netti Farmhouse before they are stranded separately.

First up on Fred's plan: Kitt. He goes to the master suite, goes to the window, and pushes aside the room darkening verticals. Kitt groans, then whimpers.

"Kittridge."

"Whaaaat?"

"There's a situation. I need you to get up, throw some clothes and things into a duffle, take a two minute shower, get dressed, and meet me in the kitchen in fifteen minutes. No questions. Move."

She does as she is told.

Next up on Fred's plan: Callie and Tess. Fred knocks once on each closed bedroom door, and flicks on the hallway lights. Twin groans come from the faux twins.

"Callie. Tess."

"Whaaaat," they whine in unison.

"There's a situation. I need you to get up, throw some clothes and things into a duffle, take a two minute shower, get dressed, and meet me in the kitchen in fifteen minutes. No questions. Move."

The girls do as they are told.

Next up on Fred's plan: Cluster. Fred places the call and waits through hideous music until Cluster answers. Fred doesn't engage in pleasantries. "Cluster, there's a situation. I need you to get to Cutters as soon as possible. I need you to get Annie and Mike and bring them to Netti Farmhouse. Mike can fill you in when you get them. Arm yourself, and expect to be with us until the storm is over. I'm sending two patrol cars as back up. Pull as close to the door as possible. Do not get out of your vehicle."

"On it Detective."

"Another thing, get rid of your damn cell phone music."

"On it Detective."

Next up on Fred's plan: Mike and Annie. Fred places another call, "Monopoli. You two ready?"

"Yes, Detective."

"Cluster is getting you two and taking you to Netti Farmhouse. His ETA is twenty minutes, give or take a few for the snow. Can you see the parking lot from your side of the building?"

"No, but I can watch from Sneade's place across the hall."

"Good, get in place. See you, soon."

When Kitt and the girls arrive in the kitchen, the detective pulls rank, explains the situation, and sets expectations. "Tess, there has been some blowback from the Hector situation. There are some people who are pissed that he is dead, and they have set their sights on you."

"There **was** someone at the cemetery?" the teen chokes.

"Yes." He goes to Tess, and wraps his arm around her shoulder. "We need to make sure you remain safe and we will." He gives her shoulder a little squeeze. "I promise, Tess."

She nods, and smiles.

He addresses Callie, "Because you look exactly like Tess, we need to set safety measures for you too. We are getting into the RAV4. You two are to sit on the floor in the back. Do nothing, say nothing, until you are safely in the farmhouse. Get your things."

Fred places his hand on Kitt's baby bump, "And you two. How are you doing?"

In spite of it all, Kitt smiles wide, "Your son and I are great."

"Son?"

"You've been right so far, so I figure…"

"A boy!" He beams.

That's the spinster?

Silence fills every inch of the BMW. Twenty miles from Mayflower, John breaks the silence. "I crossed a line that I shouldn't have crossed, Roni." He is met by her continued silence. "I'll probably cross it, again."

Mike and Annie knock on condo 2C— three hallway doors open simultaneously, and the hallway fills with Bodreaus, Sneades, and Bucks, oh, my!

"Michael dear, you look troubled. Should we expect a gunfight?" old lady Bodreau asks.

"Well, Annie and I are in a bit of trouble."

Sneade turns his back toward Monopoli and lifts the back of his flannel shirt. Tucked into the waistband of his jeans is a pistol. "Don't worry, Monopoli, I've got your back."

The MFPD officer **does not want to know** if the redneck is licensed to carry a concealed weapon. "What I could use right now, Sneade, is access to your place. I need to watch for our ride."

"Come on in."

Apparently, the entire hallway takes that as an invitation because everyone crams into the condo. The room silences when a knock comes on the door, and a call comes from the hall, "Hey, where is everybody?"

"I'll get the door. That's just my daughter," the old lady says.

Mike leans toward Annie, "Here comes the spinster."

A tall, beautiful woman with lion mane hair and sapphire blue eyes enters the condo.

"**That's** the spinster?" Annie croaks.

"Bodreau thinks she's a spinster. She's really a Cougar."

Annie raises a quizzical brow at her man, "And you would know this how?"

"Cougar Spinster has a thing for Speil. Apparently, he's got a thing for her," Mike winks.

Annie checks out Cougar Spinster again, "I can see it."

Three black Range Rovers with two goons in each vehicle leave Boston to assist Marco in the take down. The Miami drug lord is sending a message to the band of brothers that Paulo Montoya is the head of the new regional drug syndicate. His preferred way of getting there— upping the ante. "Marco, get the computer puta into the hands of the Montoya cartel, kill DEA Special Agent, Veronica Shields, and cause as much collateral damage as possible."

Driving is treacherous. There are accidents on nearly every road as the RAV4 inches from Laurel Falls to Mayflower. Fred has Kitt call Cluster to let him know that the patrol cars he sent can't get there. Cluster, reports back that the pickup of Mike and Annie went off without a hitch, and they are on their way to Netti. The snow is nearing ten inches deep when Steve pulls onto the farmhouse driveway, followed immediately by Fred, and Cluster bringing up the rear. John's BMW is nowhere to be seen, so Annie opens the place, her fingers flying over the keypad like a concert pianist's over eighty-eight black and whites. As soon as every level of security is dealt with, the group rushes en masse into the near frigid farmhouse. Callie and Tess grab their gear and bound upstairs to their room.

"Where's John?" Steve asks right out of the gate.

Fred answers, "On his way in from Boston."

Everyone in the room has their suspicions as to what, or who, John was doing in Boston. Everyone's suspicions are confirmed when the sexy suspects blow in on a gust of frigid, snowy air.

Nine people occupy that farmhouse kitchen without making a single sound.

One of them pretends to be an adult. "This is ridiculous." Kitt walks to the back door and extends her hand to THE MOST EXQUISITE WOMAN SHE HAS EVER SEEN. She wants to puke. Might be the effects of baby Serpico. Might be the effects of the former Mrs. Serpico. Matters not. "You must be Veronica, it's nice to meet you," Kitt million-watts her.

"It's nice to meet you too, Kittridge."

Seven people scatter from a farmhouse kitchen without making a single sound.

Kitt smiles at Fred's ex-wife, then throws her gauntlet. "I'd prefer if you'd call me, Kitt."

Veronica nods and starts removing her coat and gauntlets.

"How was the trip in from Boston?" Kitt asks, though Kitt. Does. Not. Care.

"John drove, so he'll probably sport a few gray hairs over it. I was a stoic passenger, although I did hit the imaginary brake a few times."

They laugh. A little.

Every so often, one of the very Un-Magnificent Seven strolls by the kitchen doorway checking for bloodshed.

Kitt starts toward the living room. "We should join them before they send in a spy to check things out. In this house, that's more of an inevitability, than a possibility."

They laugh. A little.

As the women step around the corner, Fred, and Steve mumble something about tending to fireplaces. John approaches Veronica and takes her to his room. Maura and Kitt head back to the kitchen to put on coffee and lay out a spread of muffins and scones. Mike, Cluster and Annie stay in the living room placing bets as to how long it will be before the shit hits the fan.

Montoya's reinforcements meet Marco at the motel. The kidnapping/hitman already sent the other two goons to do reconnaissance at the condo building and the bungalow. They reported back that a blue Jeep Wrangler pulled onto Cutters' parking lot and left with a guy and a girl. The goons followed the Wrangler to Farm Road where a black Land Rover and white RAV4 were in the process of parking. Missing from the farmhouse was the black BMW which showed up within minutes with farmhouse guy and Black Beauty.

"The computer girl, a bunch of yokels, and Black Beauty are at the farmhouse waiting out the storm. They just made my job easy," Marco laughs.

Fred calls a meeting in John's cave so he can introduce Roni to everyone. "You know my partner Steve; he will be armed. Next to him is Maura. She is our medical professional; she will not be armed. Next to Maura are Callie and Tess, they are nearly identical girls; they will not be armed. And they **will not** confuse you as to who is who. Next to them is Annie; she will not be armed. Next to Annie is Mike; he will be armed. Next to Mike is Cluster; he will be armed.

Next to Cluster is Kittridge; she will not be armed. You know John and me."

Nine adults sitting in that cave are **very** aware of how well Roni knows those two men.

Fred begins his instructions, "Callie and Tess. I speak for everyone in this room when I say that you should not be sitting here facing what might go down. Everyone in this room is committed to protecting you; that goes for you, too, Annie. Look at the adults' faces. If any one of them tells you to do something—you do it—without question—without pause. Is that clear?"

The girls nod.

Fred continues, "If something happens, it will escalate quickly. Look around this room."

Everyone looks all around.

"There are no windows in this room. This is where Kittridge, Maura, Annie, Callie, and Tess should come—at the first sign of trouble. Mike and Cluster will be in this room with you. Once you get here—you do not leave. For any reason. Is that clear?"

The girls nod.

Fred eases back his tone before finishing, "Callie and Tess, from this point on, it is the buddy system for you two. If one of you goes to the bathroom, the other one sits outside. When you come downstairs, you come together. No exceptions. Keep your clothes and shoes on, and leave your cell phones here. We'll keep them plugged in so they have a full charge. Okay girls, if you want to head back upstairs, you..."

The girls bolt from the cave.

Fred addresses John, "I mentioned to Kittridge the other day that I hate this room because there aren't any windows. She said this room had windows when she lived here."

John nods.

"Care to show me the super-spy modifications you've made to this room?"

You were standing, right?

All eyes are on John as he walks to a paneled wall on the left side of the cave. He reaches his hand to the top section of paneling and pushes downward. An almost unnoticeable click is heard at the same time an opening appears along a seam in the wood. John repeats the action on two more panels. The super-spy then runs his fingers along the seams until the weathered oak sections swing open. Inside the openings is a cache of assault weapons, handguns, and ammunition. Like magnets to steel, the law enforcers are on their feet, and are being "pulled" to the paneled opening. Maura, Annie, and Kitt escape to the kitchen.

"Oh. My. God." Maura's voice is low, but she may as well be screaming. She looks at her best friend in amazement, "How are you doing it? I mean standing in the kitchen shooting the breeze with **that** woman. You were standing, right? I mean, it was hard to tell. The woman's legs go on for days, and well your pittance of a height was very noticeable. And that face. Did you see that face? It's the face that could rule a nation, honestly, her image should be stamped onto coins or something…"

Annie smacks Maura's arm to halt the verbal onslaught.

Kitt walks away from Maura and Annie. She takes a seat on one of the club chairs on either side of the fireplace, tucks the pittance of leg God gave her beneath herself and exhales. The act seems to push any fortitude she's been faking out into the ether. Big, full tears fill her eyes and plop one by one down her flushed cheeks. Annie crouches at the foot of the chair, just as she had done hundreds of times when the Mahoney-Maxwell clan lived at the farmhouse.

"Oh, Mom. Try not to worry about Veronica."

"I'm not worried about her."

Kitt's daughter raises to her full impish height and says, "You're not!? What are you, blind? I mean have you **seen** her? Honestly, I've had to smack Mike five times already for staring at her. I told him the next time he ogles that woman, I'm smacking him in his bad shoulder. And Cluster, forget about it. The man's a pig. Just wait 'til I tell Jane about that big oaf's drooling and…"

Annie's tirade is cut short by Fred, who's come to get them. He takes one look at his woman and asks Maura and Annie to leave the kitchen. The man who used to be married to HER crouches before HER, takes her hands in his. "Kittridge. Are you alright? You're pretty red," He takes his hands from hers and runs his thumb pads across her flushed cheeks, "I'm sorry for all of this."

She silently shakes her head, "Fred, I'm fine. I don't really know what came over me.

Maura and Annie were just stating the obvious about Veronica, and I lost it. I'm fine now, really." She gets up from the chair and finds herself pulled into Fred's arms. He keeps her pinned against his chest until she pushes back and looks into his eyes, his gorgeous moss green eyes.

He brushes her hair from her face, her beautiful face, "Kittridge Mahoney, I am 100% yours. I'm still not sure why you want me, but that's a conversation for another day. I'm just so happy that you do want me."

John interrupts from the doorway, "Fred, we need you back in the cave."

Kitt pulls a cleansing breath and stiffens her spine, then walks through the farmhouse with the only two men who have ever been in her life. She tries very hard to ignore the fact that they have both been in Veronica.

The gun panels are closed by the time they get back to the cave. A similar looking paneled section on the opposite wall is open. The stunned woman watches as Mike and Annie enter the paneled section, and within seconds reemerge on the other side of the wall. Then she watches as Maura and Steve repeat the in and out move.

"Is that a room...in the wall?"

"A safe place," John answers.

Kitt walks to the opening and peeks inside. John joins her, takes hold of her hand, and leads her through. Within seconds they exit from the paneled section.

"This safe place...do you expect the girls to hide here?"

"The girls, you, Annie, and Maura, yes."

"Do you think it's going to get that bad?"

John pauses before answering, "I hope not, but the safe place is where you and the girls need to go **before** it gets bad." He pauses a very long moment and looks into her eyes, "I haven't given you any reason to trust me, but I'm asking you to try."

Kitt takes his hand and gives it a squeeze, "Partners, John."

"Always," he kisses her temple and pulls her close.

Veronica watches the scene play out. She looks at Fred, sure that she'll see something on his face that says he isn't alright with the connection John and Kitt have. What Veronica sees is complete acceptance. She whispers the undeniable truth, "They're together."

Eight goons and Marco Martinez sit in a motel room. They are filling their guns with bullets and their heads with blow. Marco explains the attack. "You five will enter Farm Road High. Get as close to the farmhouse as possible, but keep close to the tree line. My driver and I will enter Farm Road Low. You other two will move in behind us after we start toward the farmhouse. Use your vehicles to block Farm Road Low. Take out the cops when they arrive. **Midnight Massacre in Mayflower** is what this slaughter will be called."

John and Steve head to the farmhouse basement to get provisions.

"Holy crap John, this is a fully stocked bunker. You could live in this farmhouse alone for years and never need to shop."

"I live in this farmhouse alone, and I hate to shop. This is functional."

"This, my friend, is Y2K bonkers, but I love it."

The men grab cans of tuna and soda and head back upstairs.

After lunch and cleanup, Annie takes Roni, Mike, and Cluster on a tour of the farmhouse. Maura tags along.

"You've been in this house a million times, Auntie Maura, nothing's changed."

Maura smiles, "Everything has changed, Doodles," she shoots Roni a look.

Roni nods.

Maura nods.

Doodles gets the message and smirks, then she gets back to business. She starts by calling attention to the two sets of stairs leading to the second floor. "One set is here, around the corner, behind the kitchen fireplace. The other set of stairs is opposite the front door. That set is closest to the cave. On the second floor there are four bedrooms and two bathrooms." Annie knocks on the only closed door.

Faux twin voices call out. "Come in."

"We're on a tour of the farmhouse. I want everyone to know where you two are."

The teens shrug their shoulders. "Shut the door on your way out," they say in unison.

Veronica asks, "Do they always do that, you know, talk in unison?"

"Always!" Annie and Maura shout and then groan. In unison. The in sync response receives a chuckle from the tourists. Annie points out a guest room across from the girls' room, then moving down the hallway, she shows them two bathrooms across the hall from one another. "Next to this bathroom is the staircase that ends at the front door. Next to the other bathroom is my mother's master which is next to my room— the bedroom closest to the stairs." Annie whispers, "Very handy if you're planning on sneaking out at night. Watch out for the fifth step from the top, it squeaks."

The young woman who grew up at the farmhouse smiles when she steps into her former bedroom. "It's hasn't been changed at all since I lived here, so yes, I'm to blame for the color carnage." Beige walls are cut with burnt-orange diagonal stripes that match the bedquilt her Nana Maxwell made her. Black throw pillows and a shaggy black and orange polka dot scatter rug finish the look. "School colors," Annie admits sheepishly. "Go Tigers!"

Everyone laughs at Annie's enthusiastic cheer.

"These are the colors of your Jeep," Mike adds.

"My deceased Jeep," Annie bemoans.

Maura raises an empty hand in a faux toast, "Your tiger Jeep, she did ye well. May her killer, rot in Hell."

"Hear, hear," is replied—in unison!

She said I can have you.

After the tour, everyone returns to the cave for updates. Steve takes lead. "I've been in regular communication with MFPD, specifically Officer Grant Speil. He will be updating us on emergency personnel availability, which as of now, is none. He will also update us on traffic and weather issues. I asked Annie to program everyone's cell phone—if you need emergency assistance, we have set a direct line of communication to Officer Speil. Use any cell in this room and press the number 5—your call will go to Speil at MFPD. Calling 9-1-1 will bring you to the dispatch call center, but because of the volume of snow emergencies, 9-1-1 is your **second** option. Until we say otherwise, use number 5 for emergency-related calls. Okay, anyone with a Mahoney or Maxwell in your name, stay here for a family meeting."

Kitt's heart does a little nervous thump-thumping when she looks at her daughters. The enormity of what is happening hits hard. She pushes her hands tight against her thighs in an effort to stop their shake, only to find that the inner turmoil redirects itself to her breathing, which begins to hitch, "First, we want to know how you two are doing with all of this?"

"We're good," Callie says, turning stunned eyes at her doppelganger sister who didn't answer in unison. "Right?"

Tess pauses a minute, seemingly unsure if she should say otherwise. "Well, I'm actually a little scared. I feel like I did that day at the cemetery, sort of freaked out. But maybe it's the mouse. That whole mouse in my bedroom thing, that was terrifying! So, I'm not feeling like that, but I'm still scared."

"What mouse?" John asks.

"The one Fred was looking for under my bed," Tess answers. "You haven't heard about the mouse?"

"I'll fill you in, later," Fred says with a "drop it" tone owning his words.

John nods, then addresses his younger daughters, "Girls, do you know what my job is?"

"You're a computer geek," they reply.

"Yes, but I also work for the FBI."

"You're a spy?" they ask.

"Sort of." He gets up from the couch where he's been sitting with the girls. "Callie and Tess, come here."

They do as they are told, and cross the room as though they are super-glued together, then stop on a dime. Their mouths drop open when John reaches above a section of paneling and opens a secret door. John motions for the girls to enter the safe place. The girls do as they are told.

"This is sooooo coooool," Callie and Tess squeal from inside the cramped quarters.

"Girls," John says in his dad voice, "this can be cool, later. Right now, this safe place could save your lives. Come out. Look at me. If anything happens—if anyone gets into the farmhouse—you get to this room. Whatever adult is in this room will tell you to get into the safe place. You are to do it immediately. You will not talk—you will not laugh—you will not make any noise once you are inside. You will not leave the safe place until one of us comes to get you. Have I made myself clear?"

"Yes, Dad," they reply.

Marco checks the time. Again. He checks the snow-related weather and news on the television. Again. He checks the snowing and blowing conditions out of the motel window. Again. He would call off the attack, but he's already heard from his boss five times. Paulo Montoya wants this done. Today.

"Midnight, we roll," he tells his goons before heading to his room to do whatever it is he does before a massacre.

The law enforcers meet in the cave after the family meeting disbands. There is business to discuss.

"According to Speil," Steve begins, "every cop and all other emergency personnel are out on the streets. There are accident scenes everywhere, two that are particularly bad, closing off roads. Farm Road Low is one of those roads. This might work in our favor, or against it. If Montoya's men make a move within the next few hours, they will have to come from Farm Road High. That's good because we can concentrate on that entry point. That's bad because we have limited visuals with the tree line. My guess is that they will wait until dark. The snow will be tapering off by then, and plows will be out in force. We're going to start guard duty as soon as this meeting ends. Let's do four-hour shifts. First up is Mike."

John asks Fred to hang back, as the others leave the cave.

"Is this about Roni?" Fred preempts.

John nods.

"This isn't something I need to discuss, John. I've moved on. Roni should too."

John isn't sure he is buying Fred's words, "Explain the hang up this morning."

"Look John, I'm not surprised you two went there. I was surprised that you two went there with all that's going down. Don't read anything else into it."

The subject dies in the silence of the room.

When Fred, et al started their meeting, Kitt headed upstairs to her lavender and green room to rest. She is woken by the sound of a knock.

"Come in," she says, as she sits up against the headboard.

"Kitt, do you have a minute," Roni asks from the doorway.

She gets off the bed and waves the ex-wife in, "Sure." The women square off on opposite ends of the room. Unasked questions fill the space between them. Kitt speaks first, "Veronica, did you come to Mayflower hoping to get Fred back?"

"Yes."

Roni's directness startles Kitt. Her heart picks up speed, and her hands begin to sweat. She is readying herself to tell Veronica to back off when—

"Now that I've seen Fred with you, I know I can't have him back. He has moved on—with you." The ex-wife moves farther into the room and sits on the edge of Kitt's bed. "It's hard for me to say this, but Fred is in love with you. I recognize the look when he's near you. It's a look of love and commitment. Fred had that look for me, once. I didn't always appreciate it. When Fred asked me to choose him over my job, I made the wrong choice. I knew it the second I made it, but I let him go anyway. Choosing my job over the man I love is the biggest mistake I've ever made." Roni shakes her head, "You know, that's something I had in common with Joy. I don't know if anyone told you that Joy and

I became friends while at Quantico and that we remained friends?"

"No."

"We weren't supposed to, but Joy and I stayed in touch regularly, even while she was here working the Hector case. She reached out to me—I wasn't able to get back to her before..."

Kitt is stunned into silence by Veronica's admissions and she hangs her head at the mention of Joy's name. It stays low, until...

"Joy appreciated what you did for Tess. She said that you are a wonderful mother to your girls, to Joy's girl."

A heavy silence settles between the women and holds them tight.

"Well, thank you for listening, Kitt." Roni gets up and walks to the door.

The crazy woman in the lavender and green room stops her, "Veronica, are you giving up Fred because of the baby?" Kitt realizes instantly that she's inflicted unintentional harm.

The wounded woman turns and leans back heavily against the door she'd almost made it through. When she gathers herself, she chokes, "You're pregnant?"

The expectant mother instinctively touches her abdomen, "You didn't know?"

"No, I didn't." She tries to smile, then turns and places her hand on the doorknob. She says one last thing before she leaves. It is something that Kitt never expected, and doubts she will ever forget.

"There was something else Joy said about you, Kitt. She admired how you accepted the fact that John had moved on from his relationship with you. I'm going to follow your lead and accept the fact that Fred has moved on from me."

Veronica's parting words are still banging in Kitt's head when Fred enters her bedroom. "Did I just see Roni leave?" he asks cautiously.

Kitt begins to shed the tears she'd held inside.

"Damn it, Roni!" He puts his arm around Kitt's shoulder and sits with her on the bed. "What did she say that upset you?"

"She said I can have you."

Fred laughs big.

Hooah!

Fred asks John, Steve, and Roni for a meeting of the minds. "I was thinking…"

Steve and John shoot looks back and forth. They know when Fred starts a sentence that way, anything can happen.

The detective ignores the looks, "What if we put Steve and Cluster in Netti Barn. I know Steve is a sharpshooter, and Cluster was in the Army, so he knows his way around a rifle. If they're in the loft, they'd have an elevated view, and could catch any movement coming from either end of Farm Road. Without some sort of warning, the attackers will be on us before we see them. Especially if they come from Farm Road High. There's way too much tree cover on that side of the house."

Roni and Steve start nodding.

John holds back.

Fred starts his roll again, "Montoya's men will most likely leave their cars and come in on foot when they are near enough. Maybe Steve and Cluster can take out a couple guys before they get to the farmhouse. If we get our shooters over to Netti Barn now, their tracks will be filled in before dark. No one will know they're there, until it's too late."

John expresses his concerns. "If we put two men in the barn, that leaves us with two less armed people inside the farmhouse, and Mike's injured. So, I don't know, Fred. Three frontline people, me, you, and Roni, with Mike in the cave. We don't know how many guys there'll be. We could be overpowered at the house, where the women and girls are."

"Right, but if we get the women into the safe place and put Mike in the cave as the last line of defense, the three of us should be able to handle anyone who breaches the front of the farmhouse, and Steve and Cluster will cover the back from Netti Barn." Fred gives it a minute then says, "Yes, or no."

"Yes," Steve says.

"Yes," Roni says.

"Yes," John grunts.

The men who are now on sniper duty head directly to John's weapons and ammunition panel and choose their rifles; Remington 700s for each. Steve nods. Cluster shouts, "Hooah!"

Maura and Annie pack provisions for the men and since lights are staying off at the barn they pack flashlights, cell phones, and blankets. The women watch as the men trudge through the deep snow. Annie nudges Maura, "It feels like they're going off to war."

"Let's hope not," the nurse who's fallen in love with the detective sighs.

Seven adults and two teenagers sit down for a spaghetti dinner, before the first bite, the farmhouse loses its power. Fred, John, and Roni spread out across the house. Mike presses number 5 on his cell and is instantly connected to Speil. "Grant, we just lost power at the farmhouse. Is it isolated to us or widespread?"

Everyone waits, anxiously.

"Good. Grant. That's good. Do you have any updates on Farm Road Low? Okay, we'll keep checking in." Mike announces that the power outage is widespread.

Fred bangs his shin on a table on his way back to the kitchen, "John, any chance you have candles?"

"Nope."

"Flashlights. You have flashlights?"

"I did, until you sent them to Netti Barn."

Seven adults and two teenagers dine by the light of four cell phones, before they finish, Steve calls from the barn with an update. "Nothing yet, Fred. The blackout might work to our advantage. Coming in on foot in the dark will be tough for the goons, better for us. Hey, did you know Cluster did sniper work in the Army?"

"Knew about the Army, not about the sniper work. I'm taking that news as a good sign. A really good sign, Steve."

"I hear you, Fred. I'm starting to get an itch that things are in the wind. So, if you have anything to say, say it now. The next time your phone rings, and it's me or Cluster calling, you'll know the guests have arrived."

"Good to know, Steve. Good luck out there."

"And in there," Steve disconnects the call.

Fred takes guard duty after dinner.

John assigns sleeping locations. He deems the upstairs off limits due to the power outage. He sends Tess, Callie, Annie, and Mike to the cave, and moves in one of the recliners from the living room for the injured officer. He puts Maura on the other recliner in the living room, and puts Kitt on the nearby couch, where she immediately starts to doze off—but not before she sees John take Roni to his room.

No sooner has John's bedroom door closed when Veronica begins.

"Kitt is pregnant."

"Yes."

"You didn't tell me."

John studies Roni's body language, arms folded across her chest, one hip raised slightly higher than the other, hitched breathing. Roni is pissed.

"Not my news to tell, Roni. By the way, who told you?"

"Kitt."

"Interesting."

"That's it, John? That's all you have to say?"

He steps into her personal space, runs his hands down her arms and takes her hands in his, "Roni, what more is there to say?"

Marco and his goons leave the motel at quarter to midnight. According to the most recent news reports, Farm Road Low is open, but not yet plowed. Marco's plan is to attack from both ends of Farm Road, so he doesn't mind waiting for the snowplow to do its work. The hitman and driver goon are in one vehicle, followed by two other goons in two other vehicles. They pull out of the motel parking lot behind a snowplow and follow it to Farm Road Low. The other vehicle, with five locked and loaded goons, heads to Farm Road High, where they will wait for Marco's go-ahead before moving in.

Mike kicks back in the recliner with his cell phone. He hasn't been alone in a recliner in days. He misses Annie curled into his side. He feels his woman's eyes on him, looks over and finds himself locked in her stare. She is curled onto a wood and leather club chair, her legs tucked underneath her. She is deep in thought— when she comes around she offers him the widest smile, and a, "I told you."

"Told me what?"

"That this shit fest was going to be about a Mahoney or a Maxwell."

Mike cracks up. He continues looking at his girl, whose gaze has been captured by the crackling fire. Mike knows he is in love with Annie Mahoney-Maxwell, and will do anything to protect her. The thought has no sooner crossed his mind when his cell phone vibrates. "Monopoli," he grunts.

"Mike, it's Grant. Just an FYI, Farm Road Low is open. A snowplow is gonna do a low to high pass by the farmhouse—then a high to low return pass."

"Thanks, Grant." Mike yells the information out to Fred.

The detective looks out the window—a single flicker of light catches his eye. "Mike, call Steve. Have him put eyes on the plow coming in from Farm Road Low. Tell him to only call back if there's a problem." Fred watches the plow push a path through two feet of snow from Low to High, and from High to Low.

The snowplow driver ends his backtrack run from High to Low, and stops the plow to allow three black vehicles a wide berth for a turn. The vehicles proceed to box the plow in. Driver goon gets out and approaches the driver's side while Marco heads to the passenger side. Driver goon points a gun at the driver while Marco climbs into the plow.

"This is what we're gonna do."

Light snow continued to fall as the snowplow did its first pass – and its second pass.

And its third pass?

Shit is in the air.

Fred feels **it** coming. He calls from his spot at the window, "Mike!"

"Yes, sir."

"I thought you said the plow was gonna do two runs; Low to High and High to Low."

"Yes, sir, that's right."

"The plow is headed from Low to High again. **Shit is in the air**."

Mike joins Fred at the window. He sees lights cutting a wide swath as the plow inches forward followed by a black vehicle. "I'll call Speil and..." Before Mike can finish his sentence, Fred gets a call from Steve.

"Company coming from High in a black SUV. There's another black SUV coming from Low, behind a plow."

Fred shouts out, "Roni, John, attack under way! Mike, get Kitt and Maura to the cave. Steve, give me an update."

"The High SUV is moving toward the farmhouse. It's gonna get close and have some cover from the tree line. Fred, we have the back covered. Looks like you're gonna have a lot to deal with out front though."

"Hang on, Steve. John, get the girls in the safe place. Roni, upstairs, Kitt's room, northwest corner. Watch the tree line. Move."

John ushers everyone in. Go! Go! He hands out cell phones. "Keep them on vibrate, you can use the flashlight feature inside. Find a place and sit, then no moving. And absolutely **no** talking."

Mike is in the cave watching the events unfold. He winks at Annie as she steps inside. John approaches the young officer. "You all set?"

"Yes sir."

"Anyone who enters this room without identifying themselves, shoot them."

"Yes, sir."

"Good luck, son."

John joins Fred at the front entrance. He listens as Steve's voice comes through Fred's speaker phone.

"Fred. I have a visual of the vehicle on High, but the vehicle and plow on Low are obscured."

Just then, two men come charging from Farm Road Low and kick open the front door of the farmhouse.

Steve's voice yells, "Farm High vehicle open!"

Roni watches from the upstairs bedroom as five goons exit the Farm High vehicle. Three goons cut through the trees toward the back of the farmhouse. Two toward the front. The

Special Agent sets her sights on one. Shoots. "One down, one to go." She crawls across the floor as a hail of bullets fly into the room.

The brute force of the front door bursting open caused it to swing shut. It gave Fred and John time to move in opposite directions.

"Serpico!" Fred yells as he throws himself into the cave.

"Maxwell up!" John yells as he sprints up the stairs just ahead of a barrage of bullets that tear up the walls around him.

Roni ignores everything except the lone goon still outside taking cover behind a tree. "Come on. Step out. Come on."

Steve and Cluster hear the heavy gunfire from inside the farmhouse, but concentrate on the three goons moving through the tree line. Two goons simultaneously step out into the open. Two shots ring out from the loft. Two direct hits. The goons are lifted off their feet, landing on their backs in two feet of snow. The last goon stays back taking cover behind a tree.

John sprints across the second floor toward the back staircase. He pauses, closes his eyes and listens. **Creak.** He knows that creak. *Someone is coming up the front stairs.* John backtracks, steps into the bathroom on the same side as the staircase, and waits. Footfalls. They land on the second floor—they head away from him—toward Kitt's room—where Roni is.

Veronica Shields has the lone goon in her sights when he steps from behind the tree. She fires her weapon. It's a direct hit. She immediately hears a second shot ring out. She spins in time to see driver goon falling to the floor, and John Maxwell standing behind the fallen man with his arm still raised. Roni crosses the room, kicks the goon's gun away, and checks for a pulse. She smiles big as she steps over the goon's dead body.

"Come on, back staircase," John says as he takes her hand.

The mastermind behind **Midnight Massacre in Mayflower** is seriously fucked—and he knows it. Sirens in the distance tap into a sense of urgency, and tell him all he needs to know, time is not on his side. The hitman no longer cares about Paulo Montoya, or the computer puta, or which twin is the right twin, or about Black Beauty. When resignation hits—it hits hard. "I'm a dead man. I either die in Mayflower or Miami. Fuck it," he screams as he bursts into the cave.

Mike and Fred unload their weapons as soon as the "fuck it" goon charges the room. Within seconds, it is over, and it did not go exactly as Marco Martinez had planned. Tess

Maxwell, Annie Mahoney-Maxwell, and Veronica Shields are all safe. There is no collateral damage. There is, however, a dead goon lying prone in the cave. A soft glow from a beautiful fieldstone fireplace illuminates the deceased Floridian while big, fat snowflakes continue to fall outside.

Fred goes to shake Mike Monopoli's hand, "Nice work, Officer."

"Right back at you, Detective."

Mike covers the dead goon with a blanket. Fred goes to the **very** safe place, ushers everyone out, pulls Kitt into a tight embrace, and whispers, "Don't tell a single soul, but I fucking love this cave! By the way, Happy New Year."

Kitt gives her man a million-watt smile and a playful nudge, "I think I'll join you on your swim tomorrow."

Fred places his hand on their baby bump, "How about we hit the sheets wearing a jacket, some socks, and some mittens, and see what happens."

"Mittens! Happy New Year to me!"

The first day of August.

Fred Serpico and Kitt Mahoney wheel their newborn bundle out of Mayflower-Falls Regional Medical Center on what promises to be a scorcher. Waiting to share in their joy are Callie and Tess who hand their mother two dozen Smiley Face balloons – Annie and Mike who present the newborn's father with a tiny computer loaded with all sorts of kid's programs – Maura and Steve who present Kitt with a bottle of her favorite Moscato, and a happy announcement that, "There's a case at Bullet Bungalow." Also present at the introduction ceremony are another group of new "family" members, Cluster and Jane, who have fashioned everyone with party hats and blowers that remain quiet around the newborn, and Officer Grant Speil and his Cougar Spinster who are holding hands and several bouquets of wildflowers for the new mom.

On the ride home from the hospital, Fred puts on a Beatles playlist that he made: *Something. I Want to Hold Your Hand. All My Loving. And I Love Her. Love Me Do. I Will. Here, There and Everywhere. In My Life.*

Kitt beams from ear to ear, "These are all love songs. Fred Serpico, I do believe that you are smitten with me."

"Kittridge Mahoney, I believe that I am."

Kitt sighs when they arrive home. It is a sigh full of contentment. She wraps her arm into the crook of Fred's elbow, as he carries their newborn son, Joseph Mahoney Serpico, down to the shore at Bullet Bungalow.

"I want to introduce our son to your ocean, Ms. Mahoney."

Joseph, named after Kitt's grandfather, will always remind her how one act can affect the course of a life. Her grandfather bequeathed the bungalow at Laurel Falls to her with the belief that land ownership would settle her. Standing at the shore of *her* ocean, holding the hand of the man she loves, who is holding the creation of their love has settled Kitt in ways she'd only ever dreamed of.

Fred hands Joseph to his momma and sweeps her windblown hair from her beautiful, beaming face. He looks so deeply into her eyes that she feels the searing of their souls. Her man reaches into his jeans pocket and removes an enormously gaudy, perfectly ugly diamond ring and holds it out to Kitt. She hates it. He can tell.

"You don't like it?"

"Fred, it's just awful."

He laughs big. "Don't worry Kittridge, that's just the faux diamond." He reaches into his jeans pocket again. "This is the real diamond." Fred places a beautiful cushion cut diamond onto her ring finger.

He doesn't need to ask.

A touch on his shoulder.

  John and Roni started a thing after the shootout at Netti Farmhouse. FICA sent him to New York to work with the DEA on the Montoya and Hector cases. The Special Agents spent months working together, and tearing up the sheets. He has spent the last week with Roni in Seattle dealing with the question of what's next.

  John is determined not to make the same mistake twice. "Roni, I'm at a place in my life where I know what I want, or more precisely what I don't want. I don't want temporary, or 'look me up when you're in town'. I want something that might lead somewhere. I don't know if I can get somewhere with you, but I don't want to spend any more time playing games. Think about what you want. If you want to give us a try, a real try, you know where I'll be."

  John kisses Roni with thoughts about the future.

  Roni kisses John with haunts from the past.

France

Three days after John arrives in Nice, he finds himself at a sidewalk café, his mind is tortured by thoughts of Roni while in a place he should be with Joy. It's August, and Nice came after

Madrid on their alphabetical reunion list. He doesn't know why he came to their place, but he did. He is just about to leave the café when he feels a touch on his shoulder.

"I knew you'd come."

John's heart thumps an erratic beat

because he knows—

Joy is alive.

The End

More to come …

Please enjoy the teaser for my next book in the series,

They Run…

THEY RUN

THE DIRECTOR

--- PULLING THREADS ---

Book Four

SHERYLL O'BRIEN

Before he knows.
August

John Maxwell was more than halfway through his 12-hour flight from Seattle to Paris. The Mach-speeding tin can in which he sat shimmied and shook, then banged his whiskey over the sides of his glass. He lifted his now-empty tumbler and tilted it from side to side at the first airborne waitress he saw, then wiped his whiskey-wet hand across his whiskey-wet jeans.

The waitress smiled and nodded.

He smirked—he thought. *He was a bit lit*—he thought.

Long-Lean-Lovely sauntered his way. "Mr. Maxwell, cocktail service is suspended until we get through this bit of turbulence."

"This bit of turbulence is responsible for my being without a cocktail and more to the point it's why I want another inebriant."

The very lovely flight attendant smiled. "Yes, Mr. Maxwell, it's a bit of a bumpy ride." She eyed the exceedingly handsome traveler, "You look as though you can handle a bumpy ride." She smiled and bent low. "As soon as the captain turns off the Fasten Seatbelt sign, I will bring your inebriant and whatever else you'd like, Mr. Maxwell." She winked—the tips of her fingers ran along his forearm and hand.

John watched the willowy, ginger-blonde, emerald-eyed, "sure thing" sashay away. *She moves like Roni*, he thought. *She sounds like Joy*, he tried not to think. The first-class passenger reclined and willed himself to sleep.

Big mistake…

"Move," the spitfire young woman with cropped blonde hair and piercing blue eyes demanded as she approached him at his computer terminal. He laughed. "I'm not having the baby," she said when she walked into their dorm room holding a pregnancy test. He did not laugh. "You can't force me to have a baby," she said as she walked out on him. He threatened that he would.

The dead woman taunted him from the grave. "I was Joy Ann Watts. I was Dead On Assignment. I was DOA. I was a ghost. I had no value to them. You betrayed me. I took an assassin's bullet. Now I **am** a ghost."

He startled awake.

ABOUT THE AUTHOR

She is not dead.

Sheryll O'Brien crafts characters without constraints. She tells them who they are, then let's them show her better versions of themselves. She gives them life and they live it beyond her wildest dreams.

Sheryll is a lifelong resident of Worcester, Massachusetts, where she is wife to the most supportive husband ever, and mother of two adult daughters, one who refuses to leave her home and the other who refuses to tell her where she lives. Of most significance, she is MammyGrams to the sweetest six-year-old, Hadley.

Sheryll worked several years in the fundraising community of Worcester County, writing grants for non-profit organizations. She began writing for her own pleasure after surviving brain surgery and breast cancer. Happily, for her fanbase of family and friends——she is not dead.

If you have enjoyed reading my book, I would very much appreciate you taking a few minutes to write a review and post that review on amazon.com and goodreads.com.

The opinion of readers can help prospective readers make a purchasing decision.

To learn more, please visit my website, www.pullingthreadsnovella.com and subscribe to my blog for updates on future projects.

I would absolutely love to hear from my readers, you can email me at, pullingthreadsnovella@gmail.com

www.ingramcontent.com/pod-product-compliance
Lightning Source LLC
Chambersburg PA
CBHW070826180626
46818CB00001B/408